Murder at Mama Gene's

Rachel Pinder

Published by Rachel Pinder, 2022.

This is a work of fiction. Similarities to real people, places, or events are entirely coincidental.

MURDER AT MAMA GENE'S

First edition. February 1, 2022.

Copyright © 2022 Rachel Pinder.

ISBN: 979-8201060473

Written by Rachel Pinder.

Table of Contents

Chapter 1
The Unexpected Incident

Planning the murder had been a delicate and demanding matter. Stella examined her watch and the darkening sky outside of her car window. It was time. She didn't want to scare the children, nor could she chicken out. With one hand, she unbuckled her seat belt. "Let me out."

"Mom, it's too far." Felipe kept his eyes on the road.

"It's okay. I'll walk." She pointed to a stop sign on the corner of the dirt road. She didn't want her kids going anywhere near that blasted hotel.

"We're leaving soon. Why does it matter?"

"Let me out!"

"Mom," Lupe said, staring at her with wide eyes, "it's too dark and cold."

Stella tapped on the back of the driver's seat. "I'm late for work."

"All right, all right," Felipe relented. "You wanted to take these back roads."

The brown Buick sprayed gravel as Felipe pulled off to the side of the road. Stella's purse rattled as she closed the car door behind her.

In the front seat, Lupe rolled down her window.

Stella bent down to meet the gaze of two worried teenagers. "No TV. Homework."

"Okay." Felipe rolled his eyes.

Lupe reached for her mother and placed a hand over Stella's tanned fingers. "Think you'll get in trouble?"

"I'll be fine." Stella gently pulled away.

"But—" Lupe gulped. "What if *he* calls again?"

"Don't worry." Felipe stroked his little sister's pink coat. "I won't let anything bad happen to you."

"Listen to your brother." Stella looked Lupe directly in the eye then glanced at Felipe, who gave his mother a wink she found less than reassuring.

Stella huffed. She'd worked to keep her kids in the dark about the details, but she knew Felipe had an inkling as to why they were suddenly relocating to California. He had come close to uncovering the expensive camera, so she'd had to give it back. She hoped she could count on her son to obey—this plan was their last hope. "Quit playing around, Felipe. This is serious."

For a moment, Felipe's smile faltered, and he nodded. As Lupe slowly rolled up the window, his cheery demeanor returned. He playfully mouthed "California" in his mom's direction. The old car pulled back onto the road.

Stella straightened her hat and put on her knit gloves. Without looking back, she hustled through the grass until she came to Curry Street Crossing. There, she leaped onto the sidewalk and doubled her pace. By the time she made it across the bridge and through the woods, her heart was pounding in her chest. Stella paused behind the old hospital sign, just two hundred feet or so away from the hotel.

Just one phone call left to make. Stella pulled her Motorola phone from her pocket, punched in the number, then brought the device to her ear.

A voice on the other end answered. "Hello?"

She spoke under her breath. "It's me. I need to see you."

"Do you have something already?"

"Yes." She exhaled, hoping he wouldn't see through her. "Come after eleven, and I want cash this time." Stella flipped the phone shut.

Quickening her pace, she made it to the hotel's front stoop then paused for a silent prayer. *Lord, please forgive me for what I must do. Protect me now. When it's over, I promise to find a more honest way to pay my debts. I'll go back to church. I'll send the kids to Sunday school. Things will be different for us in California. Amen.*

She opened her tattered leather purse. Just like the rehearsal, she loaded her Glock, screwed on the silencer, carefully tucked the gun into her back pants pocket, then zipped up her purse.

Stella twisted the rusted metal knob of the front door and swung it open. She barely got one foot on the shag carpet when a dimpled young man in a brown leather coat stormed past her through the door.

"Took you long enough," Will said. He marched through the parking lot to his Jeep. After slamming the door, Will's tires screeched on the pavement, and he was gone.

At five past ten, Stella placed her purse on the old wooden desk. She could smell Mama Gene's cotton-candy perfume behind her right way.

"You're late!" the old woman shrieked.

Stella removed her hat and gloves. "Traffic."

"Well." Her boss's broad shoulders shrugged under a floral apron. "Will had to cover for you."

Stella ran her fingers through her short dark hair. "I'll come in early my next shift."

"That'd be fine, plus the double tonight."

Last month, Stella had promised to cover Will's night shift. He'd probably rushed off to pack. It afforded the perfect opportunity to straighten up *all* her affairs. Everything was going according to their plan.

Mama Gene nodded with such force that her tall red wig almost toppled off her head.

When the human tornado turned downwind, probably for another cigarette out back, Theresa crept down the old wooden stairs. "She gone?"

Stella unbuttoned her navy-blue coat and carefully slid it off her shoulders. She walked over to the hall closet and pulled out a hanger. "You're safe."

Theresa scooped up Stella's hat, gloves, and purse then handed them over with shaky hands and a phony smile. The wedding band was missing from her ring finger.

Trying to avoid eye contact, Stella put the rest of her things away and flattened the collar of her blue blazer. She couldn't allow herself to feel guilty or remorseful.

"I'm glad you're here." Theresa adjusted her glasses. "Will spent the last hour doing his hair."

"It's tough being the prettiest girl in the show."

"Funny." She giggled nervously. "But seriously, I think they're going to fire him."

Stella crossed her fingers at that. "Doesn't matter though. He'll probably always have a job here."

Theresa's long sandy-colored hair covered her face as she shook her head. "He spent half the day crying on the phone. He's been fooling around backstage."

Stella leaned in. For everything she was about to take from the woman, she owed her at least one good piece of advice. "Mind your own business."

The back door screeched open. Mama Gene's heavy footsteps pounded through the kitchen and back into the lobby. Theresa grabbed a rag and began dusting the counters and lamps at once. Stella only pushed her shoulders back. She turned to see Mama Gene tuck a cheetah-print phone into her pocket.

"Tessie!" their boss bellowed.

Theresa turned and casually smiled. "Yes, Mama Gene?"

"I need to go." Mama Gene walked to the closet and pulled out her coat. "Stay until Aaron comes in."

"I'm sorry." Theresa tiptoed forward in dark flats. "I can't wait long. I have a date with my husband."

A knot twisted in the pit of Stella's stomach. Theresa's husband wouldn't be able to make it for their date or return home.

"If you leave, you're fired." Mama Gene took off her apron and slipped on her coat.

"Please," Theresa said, inching closer, "Rog and I are trying to get the spark back."

Stella's eyes fell to the floor. There would be no spark for either of them. Stella was about to put a hole in Roger Turner's head.

"He can wait," Mama Gene snapped. "Tell the therapist that she can wait too."

The twenty-five-year-old mumbled something as she twisted the life out of her rag.

If they were as far as seeing a therapist, that would explain Theresa's missing wedding band.

After firing off more duties for Stella and Theresa like setting up for breakfast, doing the laundry, and filing receipts, Mama Gene glared at the clock above the desk. She grunted, threw her hands in the air, and fumed off.

As the door banged shut, Theresa plopped down on the lobby's bench. "She never even says thank you."

"She pays in cash." Stella organized the pens and paper.

"As soon as I get enough for the divorce, I'm done." Theresa rested her head on the pastel wallpaper.

Seems like therapy is a lost cause anyway, Stella thought, soothing her nerves. She didn't want ruining a marriage on her conscience.

"How much more do you need?" Stella asked. Not that it really mattered. Theresa could use her savings to buy a black dress, pay for funeral expenses, or get herself a new life somewhere else.

"Let's not even go there." The soon-to-be widow tilted her chin forward. "And what about you? What are you saving up for?"

"Me?" It wasn't as though she could tell Theresa about taking what her husband owed her, the hitman she needed to hire, or fleeing to California. Taking Turner out was the easier part of her plans. "Keep feeding my kids. Put a roof over their heads."

"You're lucky to have them and no husband."

"I lost my husband years ago when Felipe was just a baby."

"Oh, I'm sorry. I've been here three years, and I really know nothing about you." Theresa patted the wood. "Come. Sit. Tell me about yourself."

Stella trudged toward the bench then kicked off her well-worn boots as she sat. "What is there to tell?" Stella rubbed her feet and ankles. "I wanted to give my kids a better life, and here I am."

"How many kids do you have?"

"Two. A boy and a girl."

"I want to be a mom like you, go into the new millennium with my only little nugget." Theresa paused. "What was it like for your girl when her daddy passed?"

"I found out I was pregnant with Lupe after the funeral."

"Must have been tough on your own." Theresa nudged Stella's shoulder in a rocking motion. "So, do you have a boyfriend?"

"No." Stella exhaled. "Never again."

The front door blew open.

"Hello!" Aaron sang out from the corridor. "Sorry I'm late."

"We're in here," Theresa replied, smoothing out the wrinkles on her pants. She hissed into Stella's ear, "Did you know he was married before? Still has her ring. It's totally fake—cubic zirconia."

Stella, who was already regretting their private conversation, warned Theresa again. "Mind your own business." Bad things would soon befall that foolish woman if she couldn't keep her mouth shut.

Aaron's lanky form and red hair appeared in the lobby.

"You're free." Stella sighed and patted Theresa's arm before putting her black boots on.

"I wish." Theresa frowned.

It was only a matter of time.

As Aaron walked to the front desk, Theresa followed behind him and grabbed his hand. Aaron pulled her close and whispered something in her ear. A moment later, Theresa's jaw dropped, and she placed a soft hand to his chest.

Stella pursed her lips. Roger Turner had been willing to pay her a substantial sum for a picture of his wife like that.

Aaron must've noticed Stella's look because he took an elephant-sized step back from Theresa. "Good night."

Theresa tightened the belt of her leather coat then departed.

Once it was just the two of them, Aaron turned to Stella. "Captain, where do you want me?"

"I'll work in the kitchen." Stella moved past him, ignoring the nickname. Mama Gene had called her that just one time two years ago, but the name had stuck. "You straighten up out here and file the receipts."

"Giving me the tough job, I see." Aaron took off his blue coat with silver buttons. His looks were improving since he stopped dyeing his hair black and trying to straighten it.

"I can trust you, can't I?"

"Of course."

"I'm going to need your help on a special project." Stella had to stick to the plan that she and Carmen had come up with. She needed to stay focused on her task.

"Okay. What is it?"

"I'll explain later."

"Okay, Captain," he said with a salute. The new golden watch that he'd purchased himself just after Christmas was missing.

"You know what else, Aaron? You should be careful with that girl."

"I know." He frowned. "I'm trying."

"Good." Stella moved to meet his gaze. "We all have our reasons for working here.

Aaron nodded.

Stella could tell it was a sign of his surrender. It had taken her about a year to learn to read him pretty well. And tonight, her only friend and the best colleague to ever work night shifts with would have to help her hide the body.

Before making her way into the kitchen, she warned, "Try harder."

Aaron worked the front desk as usual. Stella found reasons to repeatedly pass by the threshold, waiting for her target to arrive.

After fifteen minutes or so, a pair of heels clattered across the corridor. Stella peered over the door and saw Will sprinting toward the desk in a sequined dress.

"What are you doing here?" Aaron asked.

"I forgot my bag." Will panted as he leaned on the breakfast table. He kicked off his heels. "You look like shit."

"You're a fine walk to talk, going around without a coat."

"The concealer around your eye," Will pointed to his coworker's left brow. "It doesn't match your skin tone. Where'd you get that shiner anyway?"

"Never mind that." Aaron covered his eye. "Good luck in Chicago."

"It's going to be fantastic." His blue eyes widened as he tucked his heels under his arm. "We're leaving tonight." After wiping sweat from his brow, Will silently loped up the stairs.

Although she'd been spying on them from the kitchen, Stella called, "Is someone there?"

"Just Will," Aaron replied. "He forgot something."

"Help me for a while." Stella wanted another look at Aaron and his black eye. She didn't know how she'd missed it earlier. Too distracted, she supposed. "The tomatoes need slicing."

"Coming." Aaron closed the notebook and register drawer. He went into the kitchen and helped her prepare breakfast.

A few minutes later, someone rang the bell at the front desk. Stella intended to go, but Aaron beat her to it.

A petite woman wearing all black and dark sunglasses stood in the lobby.

"Good evening." Aaron's black sneakers squeaked as he hurried behind the desk. "May I help you?"

Her fit little waist shifted as her hips moved from one side then the other. She rested an elbow on the desk, revealing an empty blue duffel bag wrapped around her arm. "I need a room, please."

"Smoking or nonsmoking?"

"Smoking."

"Queen size or two twins?"

"It doesn't matter. I won't be here long." The woman looked at her cell phone. "I just need the room for about three hours. Can I get half price or something?"

"Sorry. Our rates are fixed. Sixty-nine dollars per night."

"Hey." She leaned in and pointed directly between Aaron's eyes. "Do I know you from somewhere?"

"I don't think so."

Stella lingered near the lobby entrance and picked up on Aaron's slight tremble as he spoke.

"Yes. Yes, I do." The stranger snapped her fingers. "You play the violin at the bus station sometimes."

"Uh, yeah." Aaron looked uncomfortable, but he didn't blink once, which told Stella he was being truthful.

"Oh, it was terrible when that man slugged you like that." She ruffled through her pockets and large purse. "Do you need a lawyer?"

"No, thank you, ma'am." Aaron rubbed the side of his neck, a tell that he was lying. "I'm fine. But if my boss hears that I've been in a fight, then..."

"Say no more." She reached into her leather bag and pulled out a bundle of cash. "A room with a sturdy lock. Those folks in the parking lot must be staying here too."

After counting the cash, Aaron pushed a shabby guestbook across the desk.

"What's this?"

"Our guestbook." He slid the money into the cash register. "State law requires that you sign in."

The woman carefully thumbed through the pages and laughed. "Oh my. Robin Hood, Dorothy Gale, Sherlock Holmes, and King Kong have all been here."

Stella squinted. *Who is this woman?*

"So, who will you be tonight?" Aaron offered her a pen.

The woman paused. "I'm not sure."

"Hmm." Aaron paused. "How about Alice in Wonderland?"

"No." The woman grabbed the pen and scribbled on a blank line. "I've got a better one." When she was finished, she slid the book back across the desk and chuckled.

"All right, Ms. White." Aaron handed her a key from the cupboard. "Suite number four. It's just up the stairs and to the left."

Key in hand, she inquired, "Do you have an elevator?"

"Sorry. It's out of order."

"Thank you." The woman meandered toward the stairwell. "The middle of nowhere, no elevator, silly guestbook. Where am I?" She mounted the stairs and disappeared.

AROUND QUARTER TO ELEVEN, the bell on the desk gave another sharp ding. Stella darted out of the kitchen. There was Roger Turner. *Right on time.*

Aaron greeted the large balding man with a grumpy disposition and a brown suit. "May I help you, sir?"

With her view from the stairwell, Stella rested an arm on the railing and clocked her target. Soon, she would put a bullet in Turner's head and bury him out back. She exhaled and tucked her gun into her waistband. It wasn't that she was afraid to take the shot then and there. She just wanted to make sure that Aaron was prepared to handle everything on his own tomorrow first.

Aaron smiled from behind the front desk. "Sir?"

"Uh, y-yes," the man stammered. "We'll need a room."

"Smoking or nonsmoking?"

Stella froze as Turner glanced around the lobby and spotted her on the stairs.

He frowned and waved off Aaron's question. "Hold on. I'm not quite ready."

"Oh."

Stella pretended to scratch her lower back, running a few fingers across the loaded weapon. *Soon. Tonight.*

"I'm waiting for someone." The old man picked up his battered leather briefcase beside him. Stella's money had to be in there. "A friend. Mind if I just sit a while?"

"No problem." Aaron extended an arm to the parlor. "You can wait in there."

He mouthed a "thank you" then slowly dragged his feet over to the parlor.

Aaron returned to the kitchen while the old man progressed to the parlor. Their eyes remained locked on each other until the last possible moment.

Does Aaron know Theresa's husband too?

Stella and Aaron returned to their tasks without exchanging a single word. Stella's mind churned with excuses to delay the inevitable—work, the kids, Aaron needed to be prepped. *Rushing in would ruin everything. I still have plenty of time.*

She and Aaron went back and forth from the lobby to the kitchen, setting up for another day. Stella arranged breakfast dishes then packed coffee pots. She watered the plants, filled sugar bowls, then folded the clean sheets for delivery in the morning. As was their custom, one of Aaron's classical stations filled the air as they chatted. Aaron swept by the foyer and ran the vacuum. He dusted the bookcase and the banister. He polished the silver and set out tea bags.

As the moon began to rise, Aaron moved toward the parlor with a glass. Despite Stella's insistence that he keep his distance, Aaron seemed determined to offer Turner some water.

Stella was determined too. *Follow the plan—kill Roger Turner, get the money, then disappear forever.*

Chapter 2
11 p.m.

In the kitchen, Stella hid the Glock underneath a rag then rolled the silverware. After she finished, she would shoot Roger Turner and mop the floors. At least that would save her from having to clean them twice. *Ah, and defrost the bagels.* It seemed like her to-do list kept growing. *Hmmm, maybe Aaron can do that while I bury the gun out back.*

A heavy thud on a wooden surface accelerated her pulse.

Stella glanced toward the door and stuffed the gun into her back pocket. As she crossed the threshold into the lobby, she caught Aaron turning down the lights in the parlor before heading out.

"What are you doing?"

"Nothing." Aaron rubbed his neck but kept one arm behind him. "I thought I heard something."

"And?"

"I should get started on the wake-up list." Aaron attempted to hustle past Stella, but she blocked him.

She tapped the water bottle he held in his hand. "What's this?"

"This?" His hand moved forward. "I watered the plants."

"You watered the plants? I just did that."

"Oh." He cleared his throat and shrugged.

"Wasn't that for Mr. Turner?"

"He didn't want it." Aaron took a quick sip.

Stella straightened her shirt. "But he wants to sit in a dark room?"

After capping the bottle, Aaron nodded and eagerly moved back into the lobby.

Stella turned the lights back on and sauntered towards the sofa in the parlor. She would tell Roger to wait, that she would be right back to speak to him. Yes, it was getting nearly that time.

"Wait! What are you doing?" Aaron called after her.

"Fluffing the pillows." Stella marched to the front of the sofa and went pale.

Aaron flew to her side.

"*Ay, Dios mío,*" she whispered while making the sign of the cross. "What happened?"

Dark blood stained the sofa. In the center of the room, facedown on the tan carpet, was Roger Turner, a knife in his back. The darkened circle on his brown suit had stopped its swelling.

Stella's foot nudged his hand, which was spotted with dried blue ink. Roger Turner was already dead. "You killed him."

"No." Aaron didn't blink. He was telling the truth again. "I found him like that. I swear!"

The back of Roger's arms and wisps of gray hair stretched out like branches. A puddle formed between his legs. From the slight scent, she could tell it was urine.

"Okay." She patted Aaron's arm. "Let's bury him out back and forget all about this."

"We have to call the police."

Stella suppressed a smile. "You call them."

"You don't understand." Aaron's voice cracked. "I-I can't."

Stella firmly cupped his arm. "It's the right thing to do."

"I know, but I can't." Aaron pulled away. "You make the call."

"Me?"

"Yeah." He inched forward. "Tell them you went to fluff the pillows and found him like that."

"No. I'm sorry, but—"

"Please call. I'll be outside in the woods." With his head low, Aaron returned to the lobby.

"Stop." Stella followed behind. *For the kids.* She met his gaze and put a hand to her chest. "I can't call them either."

"Then what do we do?"

Stella exhaled. Best to play along until she could convince Aaron to see things her way. "Let's start by finding out who he is... was."

"Okay."

"Did he check in?"

"You saw him. He was waiting for someone."

"Did anyone come down or ask to see him?"

Aaron shook his head. "I'm not sure."

"What about a name?"

Aaron's red hair dripped with sweat. "I don't remember."

Stella pulled her shoulders back. "Then we look for ourselves."

"What?"

"We search him." She pointed toward the parlor. "Let's find his wallet."

"Maybe we shouldn't touch the body. You know, fingerprints?'

Stella gently nudged him. "I'll be right behind you."

Aaron walked over to the lifeless body in the center of the room while Stella trailed behind. When their shadows washed over the body, Aaron's finished the water in his hands.

"Check his pants and jacket."

"Me?" His eyes almost jumped out of their sockets.

"You found him."

After a deep sigh, he grabbed a pair of latex gloves from the cleaning supply box on the top of the bookcase. Kneeling, Aaron searched the dead man's coat and pants pockets. Careful not to disturb the knife, which Stella could tell had not come from Mama Gene's kitchen, he reported no lumps or bumps.

The bell at the front desk rang. "Hello? Hello?" A monotone voice called out. "Is anyone here?"

"Coming!" Stella spotted Turner's open briefcase leaning against the sofa and unzipped it. She frowned. It was filled with little white papers. *Where is the money?* He was supposed to pay her. She slammed it shut then skirted over to the front desk to deal with the impatient guest.

After giving the customer an extra towel, she stuffed the Glock back into her purse before returning to Aaron in the parlor. "Are you sure he didn't say anything?"

"It looks like he was in contact with a lawyer by the name of Nicholas Lavelle." Aaron held out the business cards he'd found.

Nicholas Lavelle? She'd seen that name before on the checks Turner had paid her with.

Aaron straightened the dozen business cards in his hands and placed them inside the briefcase. Then he grabbed the sheet of paper facedown on the floor. It looked like a fax receipt.

Stella scanned the sheet over Aaron's shoulder. Someone named Valerie Marzo had faxed twenty-five pages yesterday. The letterhead was from Turner's law firm, which included the name Nicholas Lavelle in the heading. The two men must have been colleagues and partners in keeping tabs on Theresa. That made sense. Without a word, Aaron folded it and placed it back into the briefcase.

"Come on, Aaron. Think. Are you sure he didn't say anything?" Turner was dead, which was fine. Nonetheless, Stella needed that money so the hitman would take out Marco and save her children.

"You were there, too, remember?" Aaron zipped the briefcase then leaned it against a chair.

Whatever Valerie Marzo had faxed Turner was none of Stella's business. More importantly, there was no cash in Turner's briefcase. Someone must've found out about it and taken it after offing Turner themselves. She had to find out who. The lives of her children were at stake.

Aaron's eyes widened. "I know who did this." He trembled. "I know who killed Rog."

"Are you sure?" Stella gripped his shoulders. "Aaron, you've got to be sure."

Aaron gave a vigorous nod. "The woman in black, suite four. She only wanted the room for a couple of hours. She must have done this while we weren't looking."

"Yes. That has to be it." Stella waved her arm. "Go. See if she's in her room."

"Huh?" Aaron's voice shook. "Why?"

"We need to know if she's still there."

"Okay." Aaron took a deep breath and removed the empty bottle from the table. "Then we'll get one of the other guests to call the police."

"What? Why?"

"Because it won't put either of us or Mama Gene at the crime scene." Aaron gently led Stella to the lobby. "We'll hide together until the police come and go."

"I'm not sure that this will work."

"Captain." Aaron gestured toward the stained sofa, a somber look in his eye. "We only have a little time, maybe a few hours, before someone else finds out."

"She could be anywhere right now." When they did find this mysterious woman, Stella didn't know if she would thank her or demand the money back.

"Take something to defend yourself. Just in case."

Stella nodded. For a moment, she regretted not having her gun on her, but she wasn't about to let Aaron know about her weapon—that would lead to too many questions. Instead, she grabbed a poker from the fireplace. She knew where her gun was if she needed it. Aaron fetched a candlestick from the windowsill.

Aaron shut off the light and closed the parlor doors as they left. In the lobby, behind the counter, he threw the gloves and empty water bottle away, burying them underneath scraps of paper.

They marched side by side, arm in arm, up the stairs. On the second landing, they made their way down the hallway. There were no traces of blood on the walls or the floor. No noise. Not even a light underneath suite four's chipped black door. Years after the hotel's fire, Mama Gene had instructed her and Will to paint the new doors all black. But now silver scratches could be seen through the cheap paint.

"What do we do?" Stella hid the poker behind her back.

Aaron let go of Stella's arm and prepared to knock.

Before his white knuckles met the wood, Stella yanked his arm down. "Let's get Mama Gene's keys from the office."

"Yes. It'll be better that way."

They walked to the end of the hall and made a left. Mama Gene's locked office was the last door on the right. Stella reached behind a nearby portrait of a butterfly for the spare key, but it was missing. *Mama Gene must've changed its hiding spot.*

"Captain?"

Stella swiveled her head to Aaron. "What?"

"It's open." Aaron turned the office knob and pushed the door just a smidge. "What about the other guests?"

"They'll just have to drink lukewarm coffee." Stella peered through the cracked door.

Will was inside, pacing in the center of the office. "Got it," he said quickly into his phone. "Never been more ready."

Stella inched back to avoid being seen. She had no idea how Will had gotten in. Only the night staff were supposed to know about the spare key, and she didn't think Aaron had told him.

Will continued to pace the office. "I'll be there."

The floor underneath Aaron creaked.

"Jeez, man!" Will hung up his phone and threw his hands up. "You scared me."

Stella closed the door behind them and laid the poker on the desk. "Keep your voices down."

Aaron placed the candlestick on the old leather chair beside the desk and stared at their coworker. "What are you doing here?"

Will massaged his thighs. "The show left without me."

"So?" Stella shrugged.

"So I needed a place to stay, and the coffee house gets locked up like Alcatraz."

"Mama Gene changed the locks two months ago." Stella furrowed her brow. "How did you even get in here?"

"My key still works." He presented a brass key from his worn sweatpants. Both it and his thinning T-shirt must have come from the lost-and-found bin. "That's not a new lock." He placed the key back into his pocket.

"At least you still have your job," Aaron added. "They'll be other chances. Can we do anything for you?"

"Yeah." He pointed to the blue plaid sofa by the window. "Leave me alone so I can get some sleep."

"No problem." Stella scanned Mama Gene's locked safe beside her desk and reached for Aaron. "We'll get out of your way."

"No." Aaron pulled away from her grasp. "He can help."

Will sucked his teeth. "What are you talking about? What's going on?"

Stella squinted at Aaron and pursed her lips in a warning look.

"What's happening right now?" Will pressed.

Aaron broke his staring contest with Stella to turn to Will. "There's been an accident."

"No." Stella frowned. "It was no accident. You should have slept somewhere else, anywhere else."

Aaron invited their shocked coworker over to the sofa. "We need your help."

Will blinked. "What do you want me to do?"

"Call 911. Tell the police that there's a dead man in the parlor. Say you found him lying there like that."

Will looked perplexed. "Someone died? Here?"

"One of the guests—"

"The woman in suite four killed him," Stella said, cutting to the chase.

Aaron nodded. "Her name is Valerie Marzo. If you call the police now, they may be able to catch her while she's still in her room."

Will looked from Stella to Aaron. "Well, I'm not calling the cops. You know what they say to people like me? They don't always help."

Aaron looked down and frowned at something on Will's arm. "Are you hurt?"

"What?" Will looked back at him with wide eyes.

"There's blood on your arm."

Stella followed his gaze. Sure enough, there was a spot of blood on Will's right wrist.

Will examined his arms, licked his fingertips, then wiped away the smudge. "Must have bumped into something."

"Okay, fine," Aaron said, and Stella recognized his forced tone. He was making an effort to sound friendly and understanding. "Come with us. Help us convince one of the other guests to make the call."

Will rubbed the back of his neck.

"No," Stella blurted. "Let's just get rid of it. We can bury him out back and clean up. No one else ever needs to know."

"That's it. I'm done." Will stood to leave. He fumbled under a chair, pushed aside a Polaroid camera, and emerged with an expensive pair of buckled loafers. "Count me out."

Stella crossed her arms. "If you leave, we'll say you did it." She stuck out her chin toward Will. He knew too well that she wouldn't hesitate to throw him under the bus.

"Let's not do this." Aaron angled between them. "We're wasting time. We'll go check out suite four together first. If we catch the killer, we can call the police."

After a tense moment, Will sighed and agreed. Stella firmly grasped the poker. Aaron found the master set of keys in the desk drawer and picked up the candlestick. Will set his possessions aside and grabbed the stapler.

Chapter 3
Midnight

After locking Mama Gene's office door behind them, the reluctant trio proceeded down the dim hallway to suite four. The air was stale and thick because the proprietress refused to ever open a window. Will's thick heels clicking against the old wood—Mama Gene had thrown out the old carpet and never replaced it—proved louder than the pigeons in the attic, so Aaron signaled everyone to stop.

"What is it?" Stella mouthed while raising her poker.

Aaron pointed to Will's shoes. "Take them off."

Will snickered. "Seriously?"

He nodded.

Will sighed before leaning against a dark-floral wallpaper to lift his foot. The stapler slipped out of his hand and crashed to the ground.

"Sorry. Sorry," he whispered while collecting it from the floor.

Stella pointed her poker at him. "Be more careful."

"Leave the shoes," Aaron warned.

Will shook his head. "Do you know how much these things cost?"

Aaron tucked the keys into his pocket and pointed down the hall. "We're not going that far."

After side-eyeing Stella, Will laid his shoes on the floor. The stapler cradled in his arms almost tipped out, but that time, he managed to catch it.

Foolish man-child. Will probably assumed that he and Stella were working together, like all those other nights. But if he had killed Turner, Stella wouldn't have lifted a finger to help.

Aaron waved. "Let's go."

Will took the lead slowly down the hallway.

After passing by brass-plated numbers seven and eight, Stella tugged on Aaron's sleeve.

He glanced at her in surprise.

"Why did you say Valerie?"

"Pardon?"

They passed by suites five and six.

"You told Will that the woman in suite four was Valerie Marzo."

"It has to be her." He shrugged. "She'd just sent him a huge document right before he winds up murdered. Maybe it was blackmail? It's the only way this makes any sense. Right?"

None of it made any sense to Stella. Valerie Marzo was connected to Nicholas Lavelle, who would sign checks for large amounts of money. And Stella needed that money more so than airing out her dirty laundry to work colleagues.

The group stopped in front of suite four. Stella thumbed to Aaron then to the door. He nodded. Stella tightened her grasp on the poker, and Will puffed out his chest. Oh, how she wished that she'd brought her gun.

The sounds of running water and the hum of the TV radiated from beneath the door. With one hand clutching the candlestick behind his back, Aaron inched closer. His knuckles raised to knock as the "Jingle Bells" tune sang from Stella's pocket.

Carmen. Stella quickly switched it to silent. After the move, she needed to convince her daughter to stop changing her ringtones. She would call her sister back soon. Roger Turner was already wiped out. Next, she needed to locate the money for the next part of their plan.

At the sound of her phone, the TV stopped. Stella thought she heard a window close and the sound of a zipper. The door to suite four flew open.

"Dear God." Will threw his hands in the air and nearly lost the stapler again.

A woman wrapped in a white towel stood in the doorway. Her jaw dropped when she saw Aaron and Will. "Can I help you?"

"Did you, uh, call for room service?" Aaron kept his hand with the candlestick pinned behind his back.

"No."

Stella tried to peer past the strange woman into the room. It looked the same as it always had, with the bed, dresser, desk, and mirror looking untouched.

Will chimed in. "Are you sure, Ms. Valerie?"

"Who are you?" The woman eyed the stapler in his hands. "Is this how you treat all your guests?"

"Ma'am," Aaron interrupted.

"What?" She refastened the dark barrette to her ginger hair.

The woman's dark clothes laid upon the made bed. Beside them, the empty bag she had brought with her was now stuffed with something. *Turner's money?*

"Have you been in your room this whole time?"

"Leave me alone." She puffed her cheeks and glared at him.

"Did you see anything or hear anything unusual?" Aaron continued.

"Go away, music man!" She slammed the suite door.

Aaron sagged his shoulders.

Stella thought about knocking on the door again. Woman to woman, she might be able to figure something out about their guest. But that would have to wait just a few minutes.

"Well, then." Will sucked his teeth and nudged Aaron's shoulder. "Someone's full of secrets tonight."

Stella took her phone out and raised a finger. "My kids."

She rested her poker on the wall, walked down the hallway toward Mama Gene's office, and found her sister Carmen's name in her contacts. Stella could feel the sting of Aaron and Will's eyes on her back. "Honey, what is it?"

"Honey?" Carmen laughed. "Did you do it yet?"

"Tell your sister she's fine. You're both perfectly safe."

"Good for you. I knew you could pull the trigger."

"Did you two finish your homework?" Stella asked loud enough for Aaron and Will to hear. "We have a schedule to keep."

"I'm on my way."

"Run the dishwasher and brush your teeth before bed."

"After I wire the money, they'll take care of Marco. They've got eyes on him already."

"Get to it." Stella slipped the phone into her pocket and forced a smile.

Will suggested that they head back to the office.

Stella waited for Will to get a bit more ahead of them and tugged at Aaron's arm. "Why did she call you music man?"

"She saw me dancing to the radio when she first checked in." Aaron was lying again. "Are your kids okay?"

"They're fine. My daughter worries about everything."

Aaron chuckled.

She couldn't understand why he'd lied to her. *And why would Will want to stay the night? Who was that woman?* So many questions. But none of it really mattered. Stella needed to get away from her coworkers, retrieve her Glock, and get her hands on that money. She was certain that it'd been in that woman's duffel bag. It seemed that she would have to kill more people. But then again, she did not have many bullets to spare.

The hotel workers returned to Mama Gene's office and closed the door. Will sat on the sofa to put his shoes on.

Aaron eyed one of Mama Gene's paintings. It was an ocean scene on a clear and sunny day, and a boy and his dog played in the waves. "I'm starting to think that you were right."

Stella grasped the poker with both hands. "About what?"

"Getting rid of the body. Maybe we should bury it."

"Good." Stella nodded. "Let's do it."

Will exhaled. He opened his mouth to speak, but a high-pitched scream tore through the air. It had come from somewhere downstairs, likely the parlor. Aaron, Stella, and Will took off in a chaotic blur.

As they ran down the hall, guests opened their doors to see what the commotion was. Will kept stopping to apologize and reassure them it was only the furnace. "It gets like that when it's too hot. We'll take care of it."

Aaron and Stella sprinted down the stairs and into the lobby with Will close behind. When they pushed open the parlor doors, they found Theresa on the floor by the fireplace, staring at the body. Will rushed in. Aaron closed the doors.

Stella put her hands to her cheeks and did her best to look surprised. "What did you *do*?"

"Nothing." Theresa used her soiled arms to push herself up. "He was there when I came in."

Aaron waved for everyone to join him at the other end of the room. The faint scent of cigarette smoke filled the air. They formed a small circle.

"My husband is dead." Theresa shivered.

Will used two fingers to point to Aaron and Stella. "They said they found him like that."

"You did?" Theresa blinked, confused.

"Yes." Aaron's forehead muscles tightened. "Wait. *He* was your husband?"

He was lying again.

Stella laid her poker down on a small table. "The killer is still here."

"Why hasn't anyone called the police?" Tears were in Theresa's eyes. She slipped her phone out of her denim skirt pocket.

"Calm down." Stella gently stroked Theresa's arm, wondering if she'd killed her husband. Perhaps Theresa knew about their arrangement and the offers. "Don't call the police. Do you know how this looks? You'll be arrested."

"Me?" Theresa's whole body shook.

Aaron embraced the newly widowed woman. "She's right. Your marriage was on the rocks. We should figure something else out."

Stella left Aaron to console their distraught coworker. She made the sign of the cross and stepped forward to reexamine the stiff.

"No need for that." Theresa wiped her tears with a sleeve. "Rog wasn't religious. He wouldn't even allow me to attend Mass."

Stella didn't know why she hadn't noticed it before, but she recognized the knife in Turner's back. The chef's knife with a silver swan engraved on the handle had come from Ammaliatore, where Roger Turner liked to buy those fancy coffees. Will also worked there.

"What am I gonna do?" Theresa was becoming frantic again.

"It'll be okay." Aaron stroked her hair. "We'll bury him out back."

Will laughed. "I can't believe what's happening right now."

"Okay." Theresa tucked the phone away. Without another word, she squatted over her dead husband and yanked the knife from his back.

Everyone gasped as the blood dripped onto the carpet.

Will balked. "What'd you do that for?"

Theresa had the bloodied knife raised to her shoulder. "He'll be easier to bury."

"Put that thing down," Stella demanded.

Theresa nodded and lowered the knife.

"What are you even doing here so late?" Aaron asked her.

"Rog didn't come home. I thought he might have come here to get me." Theresa's face went pink as she released the knife onto the floor. "I'm sorry. I thought I was helping."

Will's eyes found Theresa. "Now follow along, or they'll point the finger at you." He looked back toward Aaron and Stella. "Right, guys?"

"No. Not me." Theresa stepped backward, another round of tears rolling from her eyes. "I'm innocent!"

"Oh, I believe you." Will tilted his head in a mock display of sympathy. "But that's why you shouldn't bury the body. We should just figure out who is actually responsible. Then you can call the cops and tell the whole truth."

"Okay," Aaron said, giving Theresa a hopeful smile.

Stella wondered why Will was suddenly being so helpful. Maybe it didn't matter since Theresa's fingerprints were now on the knife. *Stupid girl.*

"Look. Let's just get this over with." Will placed one hand on his hip. "We split up and look around for clues."

"Fine." Aaron ran a hand up Theresa's back. "We'll look inside. Will and Stella, you go outside."

"No." Stella held out her palm. "Give me the keys. I'm not going out there."

Theresa attempted to wrap her arms around Aaron's shoulders. "What exactly are we looking for?"

Stella looked on in disapproval. The entire ordeal was a waste of time. Her target was dead, and she needed to look for the money.

"I don't know. Weird stuff," Will said. "Someone trying to hide."

"Exactly." Aaron shot Stella a pleading look, his eyes begging her to go along with the search. "When you see something, tell Theresa. She'll call 911, and we can leave the rest up to them."

Maybe she should go along with the plan. It would give her the chance to confront Will alone. If he had committed the crime, she guessed her money would be close by.

Chapter 4
1 a.m.

The coming of April usually marked the start of the hotel's busy season. Given all the travelers moving about, the night staff was often overwhelmed, setting up the breakfast buffet, cleaning tables, folding towels, filing receipts, and double-checking the wake-up call list. While most of the guests slept in silence, there were always a few blaring their televisions, fighting, or just roaming the halls. Yet tonight was very different.

Aaron closed the doors to the parlor without making a sound. Theresa slumped down on the bench, her head hanging low. Stella moved behind the lobby desk and began opening drawers.

"What are you doing?" Will asked.

"Finding the flashlight," she responded without looking up. "Go and get a knife from the kitchen."

"Fine," he groaned.

Theresa roused herself and stepped lightly through the room, spraying it with deodorizer.

Stella raised her arm, revealing a yellow flashlight in her palm. "Found it."

While Aaron was mesmerized by Theresa's dance, Stella set the flashlight down and moved to the closet. She slipped her coat on and stuffed her Glock in a side pocket.

The tapping of his heels on the old wooden floor announced Will's entrance. "What'd I miss?"

"What if..." Theresa mumbled. "What if someone comes downstairs while we're gone?"

"Good point. You stay here and keep watch." Aaron gave Theresa a reassuring smile as he handed Stella the flashlight. "We can both stay if you want."

Theresa nodded eagerly.

Stella clutched Aaron's shirt with her fist. She scanned the first floor and then the staircase. "Be careful."

"Yes, Captain."

"You ready?" Stella released Aaron and buttoned her coat.

"I don't have a coat," Will replied.

"You can borrow mine." Aaron pulled his blue jacket from the closet then handed it over.

Theresa groaned and mumbled something under her breath.

"Thanks." Will slipped the coat on and tucked a paring knife into the pocket. He swiftly followed Stella out the front door.

A chill filled the air. There were no lights from the road or outside of the hotel. It was too overcast to see the moon. Only glimmers of light from the guest bedrooms reflected on the ground.

Stella shook the flashlight a few times until it clicked on. "Get moving. I'll be right behind you."

Will zipped Aaron's coat up to his chin. "You go first."

"How many children do you have?" She nudged his shoulder.

"Ugh, fine." Will turned and walked down the three stone steps to the small parking lot filled with broken gravel.

Stella took a step forward then halted as she heard the murmur of voices back inside. She put the flashlight down and pressed her ear against the cold wood door.

"We talked about this," Aaron said. "We agreed to end things."

"Let's run away together. We can be free." Theresa sounded desperate. "We'll find somewhere new. Change our names and never look back."

Footsteps descended the stairs into the lobby. *What are they up to?*

Stella started when a hard thud sounded behind her down the path.

Will was on the ground. "Shit."

"Watch your step." Stella hastened to straighten him up. The copy of Mama Gene's office key had slipped from Will's pocket. Since he would live longer without it, she decided not to say a word.

"Thank you."

She picked up the flashlight from the steps. "You shouldn't be wearing those shoes for this."

"Well, thanks to Aaron, money for new boots isn't going to happen."

Stella shook her head at the accusation. Arguing with Will wouldn't help anything tonight. She pointed the light to the path in front of them. Six vehicles were in sight—Will's jeep, Aaron's junkyard recycled car, Roger's two-seater, two sedans, and a minivan.

"We should really ask guests about their cars when they check in."

Will chuckled. "Too late now."

They headed for the brown minivan with the tinted windows first. Stella moved the light up and down the van's windows, revealing a car seat, a soccer ball, a few blankets on the seats, and cracker crumbs on the floor. Nothing to explain a murder. There was also no place to hide a large sum of money.

"You know what really gets me?" Will's face was pressed against the glass, his breath fogging up the window. "Aaron. First, he wants to call the police, then he wants to bury the body."

Birds' wings flapped in the darkness. Stella moved the light to Roger Turner's white car beside them.

"He has a black eye he's trying to hide. And we all know that Mama Gene's 'cameras' are from the toy store, so they won't do us any good. Which one of you found the body first?"

Stella squinted with a tightened jaw. "Just look."

"I knew it. He did." He tapped the top of the car and peered inside.

The inside of Turner's car was clean, like new. The only thing that Stella could make out was a blue pen resting in the passenger seat. Roger must have written something down before coming inside.

As for Will, he wasn't wrong to assume the worst about Aaron. It all made sense if he and Theresa were conspiring to run away. But it also meant that they probably knew what Roger was up to and had decided to stop him.

"Think Theresa's okay on her own?" Will asked. "I mean, he picked us to do this job."

The flashlight in Stella's hand never faltered.

"Come on, Captain." Will leaned one hand on the car. "Let's check his car next."

Will marched to the other side of the lot to Aaron's car. "I mean, why does he call you that? Captain. What's with that?"

Stella followed. "You know better than to ask too many questions around here."

"On any other night, sure." Will looked back at her. "But you trust him? More than anyone?"

Stella pointed the light inside Aaron's car. She and Will bent down to look inside. A violin case and two cardboard boxes were on the floor. Photographs and books were scattered on the passenger seat. The backseat was made up with a sleeping bag and a pillow.

"He lives in his car?" Will blurted. "Did you know that?"

The blood drained from Stella's face. Then the screen from her cell phone lit up her pocket. Felipe's name flashed across the screen. She handed Will the flashlight then headed toward the woods. Will kept the beam of the flashlight trained on her back.

Stella held her phone to her ear. "I'm working. I can't talk right now."

"Mom," Felipe said breathlessly, "he's in the yard. What do we do?"

"Open the window, and put me on speakerphone." Stella's voice came out low and guttural. After what sounded like the smash of the phone against glass, she yelled, "Get off my property!"

She could make out Marco Bolzano muttering and yelling on the other end. Stella found her Glock and loaded the chamber. All the while, Will looked on with wide eyes.

She ignored him and shouted into the phone, "Leave, or I'll kill you!"

The sound of a siren blared through the speaker. Felipe got back on the line and informed his panicked mother that the man had run away when a police car had passed by their home.

"Lock the windows and the doors. I'll be home soon." And with that, Stella hung up, dropped the magazine, then cleared the rack. With two free hands again, she snatched the flashlight away. "Let's finish up."

Will slowly nodded. "Maybe I'm wrong."

Stella, still panting, pointed the light toward him. "What are you talking about?"

"About Aaron and you, this whole thing." He paused. "Maybe *you* wanted Roger Turner dead." He laughed under his breath. "Granted, Lavelle's money was great, but maybe he found out about some of your secrets too."

Stella marched on, and Will followed like a buzzing mosquito.

"I saw the camera upstairs. Turner gave it to you, didn't he? Offered you money for photos of Theresa?"

Will was dangerously close to the truth. But he also knew where most of Mama Gene's bodies were buried. Stella needed to stay focused, finish things up around there, then get home as fast as she could.

"Admit it." Will peered inside the window. "You killed Roger Turner, and you're just trying to avoid the same mistakes that made Casey disappear. That's what this is really about."

As Casey's replacement examined the black leather seats, Stella breathed a threat into his ear. "You think I don't know about you too?

I was here in January when you tried to quit. But Mama Gene wouldn't have it. What does she have on you?"

"Nothing that involves me carrying around a loaded weapon." Will pursed his lips and shot her a dirty look.

"Why are you even here tonight?"

Will touched the hood of the car. "These cars are all cold like they've been sitting here a while." He slid past her. "And the last bus probably pulled through here around ten. We should walk around the building next, by the perimeter."

Will stalked off in front of her, his hand clutched in his right coat pocket, shoulders hunched as he scanned the dark boundaries of the hotel. The glimmer of Stella's flashlight lit their way.

"The reason—" Will cleared his throat. "The reason they—the show, I mean—left without me was because of Tyson. He found out about Roger and decided that I was cheating on him." Will paused and looked over his shoulder. "I'm going to end up alone, trapped, just like everyone else."

Stella waved her hand for him to keep going.

Will followed. "Mama Gene took me in off the streets and gave me a job. I was so grateful that I did whatever she asked. That's how she pulled me in before that one very stupid mistake."

They reached the end of the lot. The edge of the dark forest was at the tip of Will's shoe.

"What did you do?" To her, it seemed likely that he'd stolen something from Mama Gene. That would explain his key and why he couldn't leave when he wanted to.

"Doesn't matter." Will turned to face her. "I didn't kill Roger Turner, and I'm almost certain that you didn't either. Cash in hand for spilling Theresa's dirty little secrets? Why would you?"

Stella took a step forward and moved the light ahead of them. "What do you want?"

Will stood shoulder to shoulder with her as they walked. "I want my boyfriend back. I want to go to acting school. I want a way out of here. Don't you?"

Stella remained silent. A new life required money. Money that Will had tried to steal from Mama Gene's safe. The light from her flashlight danced back and forth through the tall trees. *What a fool!*

"When we go back"—Will's breath created a cloud between them—"get Theresa to make the call. I'll cover for you. You cover for me."

"You're wrong about Aaron."

"Can't you see how guilty he is? He's playing us. We're out here while Theresa is by his side."

Stella sighed and peered into the darkness of the woods. *How did Marco even find them again?* The safety of her children had to remain her priority above any sentiments or friendships. She needed that money. She needed to get home. "Aaron did tell me once that he killed a woman. Said that he had to. Someone made him do it."

Will placed a firm hand on her shoulder. His chin tilted to the side, he asked Stella to shine a light in the corner where the woods and the concrete met.

Just ahead, a jumble of muddy footprints went deeper into the woods, and another headed toward the hotel. Stella sighed. It appeared as though two or three different pairs of shoes had been there recently.

"You smell that?" Will asked. "Smoke."

Why would someone start a fire?

Will bent down beside the tracks. He followed them with his fingers, drawing a line in the air to the hotel. "Looks like Aaron came out here and burned something."

"Impossible." Stella leaned over to examine the footsteps. "He's been beside me almost the entire time."

Will straightened and moved to a large oak tree nearby. After circling it twice, he laughed, leaned up against the trunk, and brushed the dirt from his shoes. "Why can't you see? Aaron is using us to cover his tracks.

This is him setting someone else up so he can keep his wealthy widow girlfriend. But we can beat him, or them, maybe, at their own game this time."

"These tracks…" Stella inched down to one of the dirty narrow footprints. "See the indent? This shoe had a high heel." Stella shined her light at Will's heels.

"Oh, please." Will scoffed. "I'm sure you and Theresa have a pair of your own."

She flashed the light at her boots. "You're the only one who was wearing them tonight."

"We still don't know where Theresa was, and her fingerprints are all over the knife anyway."

Stella glanced sideways and spotted a leather belt near some bushes. After shining the light toward it, she asked, "Did you leave that out here? I'm sure it looks very nice with that shiny dress you were wearing earlier."

"Careful, Estelle." Will snatched the belt then chucked it further into the darkness. "You're beginning to sound like that sour and manipulative hell beast we work for. Soon enough, you'll be dressing like her too."

"Don't try and change the subject."

"I'm sorry." He gently brushed Stella's shoulders. "We can blame each other all night, or we can agree to work together."

"And what about your Jeep?"

"What about it?"

"We haven't searched it yet."

"You want to see it?" He stepped aside and swept his arm toward the parking lot.

The sound of a large engine rumbled nearby. A pair of blinding headlights entered the yard. Stella turned her flashlight off as they ducked.

Will leaned into her shoulder and whispered, "The gun."

The shadow of a big car parked beside the minivan. The engine cut off, and the driver's-side door flew open.

Chapter 5
Christmas, 1997

Stella pulled her brown Buick into an empty spot. Judging by the number of cars, the mall was packed with holiday shoppers. But she was in the right place—Ammaliatore. The oversized advertisement with a picture of a cup of coffee was plastered on the side of the building. Stella pulled her cellphone from her purse. Ten minutes until five. She eyed the large cardboard box in the back seat and found Carmen in her contacts.

"Hello. Merry Christmas."

"Merry Christmas." Stella couldn't resist the urge to smile. "How's Frank and the kids?"

"We're all fine. Did you get my box?"

"Yes, but you sent it to the wrong address. My old landlord called me about it last week."

Carmen lowered her voice. "Did you get to the bottom?"

"The bottom of what?"

"The box. Go down the corners."

"Why? What's there?"

"Just look."

Stella sighed and got out of the car. *What did she buy the kids now?* She'd have to buy extra wrapping paper and tape on the way home.

After opening the passenger's-side door and placing the phone on the seat, Stella used her car keys to slice through the brown tape. Blue, green, purple, and pink sweaters were stuffed to the top. *At least she bought them clothes instead of toys this year.*

Carmen's voice called out from the speaker. "Did you find it?"

"Hang on." Pushing past the pile of fabric, Stella felt a small cardboard box in the corner. It was a toy gun wrapped in plastic. They were making these toys look more and more real. Thick and heavy too.

"Oh no." She moaned and gripped the phone. "Felipe is too old to play with this thing. Carmen, he's sixteen now."

"It's not for Felipe."

"I'm not giving this to my twelve-year-old."

"It's not for Lupe either." Carmen's voice deepened.

"Then who's it for?"

"Who's it for?" She snickered. "You, Stella."

"Me? Are you kidding?"

"Not at all."

Stella put the toy gun back in the box and closed the lid. "Don't make jokes."

"This isn't a game."

"What are you talking about?" Stella glanced at her screen. She still had about five minutes.

"The shells will come soon in a tin of pastries. The landlord will have to forward it to you again."

"Carmen." Stella opened the lid of the box and stared at the gun.

"Let's face it. You need protection, sis."

Stella stepped back and exhaled. "I'm meeting a lawyer today. I don't need your help."

"Stella, listen to me. Things could get very me—"

"I will not run from my problems again. It does no good anyway."

Carmen was still muttering when Stella closed her phone. It was time to go and meet Roger Turner anyway. She walked over to the passenger seat and pulled out her purse. After sifting through overdue bills and missing homework assignments, she found the letter that she needed. Stella locked the car door and made her way into the mall.

The tiny coffee shop was busy, but Roger was right where he said he'd be in the back corner with one broken light. He smiled as she entered. Stella peered at the chalkboard menu on the wall as she moved toward him. She didn't know how to pronounce most of the menu items. But that didn't matter. She couldn't afford a glass of water from them. Plus, the owners clearly didn't deserve her money. If they paid their workers well, Will wouldn't have needed two jobs to get by.

Stella sat down and unbuttoned her coat. Two green Styrofoam cups and a plate of cookies rested on the table between them.

Turner offered her a cup. "I got you a cappuccino."

Stella grinned and took a sip. Much too sweet. But she pretended to like it anyway. "Thank you."

"No problem." He twisted his gold wedding band. "Have you got something for me?

"Not yet." Stella took a cookie from the plate with silver swans encircling the rim.

"Okay?"

After taking a bite, Stella leaned across the table to meet his brown eyes. "I need your help."

Roger sat back in his chair. "If this is about more money..."

"No, it's not about money."

"A job, or you're getting cold feet..."

"No, Mr. Turner. Please, listen."

He crossed his arms and nodded.

"My daughter, Lupe, needs protection."

"What do you mean?"

"One day, her father—Marco Bolzano—kidnapped her right off the playground when I took my eyes from her for a second. It was hours before I got her back." Stella's eyes welled with tears.

Roger offered her a handkerchief.

"Marco sells drugs. He does terrible things. I don't know how he found us again."

"I'm sorry that you and your husband have problems."

"He was never my husband." Stella pulled the envelope from her purse. "He wants a DNA test. He's going to take her four hundred miles away from me."

"Oh, no."

Stella pushed the envelope across the table.

Roger kept his hands on his lap. "I'm a real estate attorney. I don't work cases like this." He wrinkled his nose. "Especially with children."

"Then you must know someone," she whispered. "I'm spying on your wife for you."

He shook his head.

"I made one drunken mistake after burying my husband. My only family, my sister, is in California. I barely make enough to cover my rent."

"Legal aid. Have you thought about legal aid?"

Stella stuffed the envelope back in her purse. She kept her voice low. "Mama Gene's hotel isn't exactly a place on the up-and-up." She exhaled. "I'd be lucky to get a prison sentence."

He stared at the ceiling.

"We can help each other. That's all I'm asking."

Roger scowled at Stella. "I'm sorry. I just can't."

"Please."

He threw on his coat and scooped up his briefcase. "I'm only interested in proof that my wife violated our prenuptial agreement."

Stella tried to return the handkerchief.

"Keep it." His voice lowered. "Theresa's been taking large sums of money out of our account. If you see something or can get me a pay stub, call me. I'll even get you a camera and pay double for the photos if you're up to it. But it'll have to wait until after the divorce."

"My kids would ask where I got the money for the camera."

Roger Turner left her at the table without a second glance.

Stella dried her eyes for the very last time, grabbed hold of her cup, and got to her feet. She marched to the trash can, tossed the handkerchief, and held the coffee cup over the heap. As the brown liquid streamed over crumpled cups, napkins, and wrappers, images flashed through her mind. She saw herself pointing the gun Carmen had given her at Marco Bolzano. Burying the body behind the hotel in the woods. Starting her life over again fresh. Free.

When the cup was empty, she let go. If she could get Marco to meet her at the hotel one night after Mama Gene had gone home, the rest would be simple. Aaron could help.

No. No. She had to stop thinking like that. Before leaving, Stella wrapped the cookies with a napkin and placed them into her purse. It would never work. She'd just made her troubles entirely worse by explaining them to Roger Turner.

There had to be another way. Maybe one of Lupe's teachers knew someone who could help. Or perhaps there was someone at the grocery store where Felipe worked. The answer was there. She just needed some time to think.

Stella made it back to her car. Tomorrow, she would visit the dump and drop off Carmen's box. The best thing to do would be to rip her name and address from the top and forget the whole thing.

Maybe pick out three sweaters for under the tree?

The "Jingle Bells" tune rang out. That time, it was her home number. Felipe probably wanted to know what was for dinner. That boy was always hungry, but she was glad to hear from him then.

Stella answered. "I'm on my way."

"Mom." Her son hesitated. "He's outside. He's demanding that we let him in."

Chapter 6
2 a.m.

Stella and Mama Gene walked into the lobby with somber faces. Will closed the front door behind them. Aaron attempted to greet everyone with a casual smile, piano music filling the hall behind him. His congenial air diminished when Mama Gene shouted, "Turn that music off!"

"Yes, ma'am." Will scurried into the kitchen for the radio.

Mama Gene loosened the tie of her butterfly-themed bathrobe and glowered. "What the hell has been going on around here?"

Stella opened the closet door and took off her coat. Cell phone in hand, she made sure the Glock was pushed to the bottom of her pocket and closed the door.

"What do you mean?" Aaron asked.

"I get a call in the middle of the night." She stomped one of her pink slippers and roared, "One of the guests says there's been an attack!" She shot an icy gaze toward Aaron, who stiffened. "I don't pay you to scare away my customers."

He bit his bottom lip and slowly nodded.

"Now, I'm going upstairs."

Aaron opened his mouth to speak.

She brushed a strand of gray hair behind her ear. "You got something to say?"

He handed her the master set of keys.

Mama Gene sneered. "Get back to work, or you're fired."

Aaron grabbed a rag from the lobby's desk and began dusting. Mama Gene watched him closely before turning and climbing the stairs.

Stella inched closer to Aaron. "What happened?"

"The woman in suite four tried to check out. We had to stop her. She must have called the number beside the bed."

"Okay, breathe." Although Will had almost convinced her of Aaron's guilt, that time, he was telling the truth. "We show Mama Gene everything is fine. She goes home, and we bury the body out back."

"No," Aaron said, his face resolute. "We can't let that woman check out."

There was no time to argue or feel guilty about betraying Aaron's confidence. Stella had to keep track of everyone and find Roger's missing money. "Where's Theresa?"

"Upstairs. Did you find anything outside?"

"Not very much. Footprints." Stella waited for Aaron to show signs of being scared, like a tremble or more sweat, but he remained unruffled. "What about you?"

"Nothing. There wasn't enough time."

Footsteps descended the stairs. Mama Gene and the woman from suite four were coming down.

Whatever it took, Stella needed to get Mama Gene to leave. If she found Roger Turner's body in her parlor, their boss would assume that either Stella, Will, or both of them had been involved. Then the old crone would demand hush money, which neither of them had.

When she reached the bottom step, Mama Gene apologized to the woman in black. "My dear, we hope you come again."

The woman handed Mama Gene a key. Her very toned arms carried that same duffel bag, which was stuffed with something bulky. "You haven't heard the last of me."

Stella tensed. *Is she going to walk out the front door with my money?*

Mama Gene's false grin dissolved as she squinted at Aaron. "Get my friend a coffee and some biscuits."

Stella rushed to her side with the attentive air of a hostess. She reached out an arm to the woman, offering to hold the bag.

"No, thanks." The woman's tiny feet shuffled back. "I'm in a hurry."

Mama Gene flashed another fake smile. "How about a refund?"

Aaron moved behind the desk. Stella soon followed, accidentally kneeing the duffel bag. She caught a glimpse of the contents—towels, soap, maybe a pillow—and relaxed. *So she doesn't have it.*

After Aaron returned the woman's wad of money, she breezed past Mama Gene's shoulder and headed toward the front door.

Aaron reached out to grab her arm as she whizzed by, but Stella nudged him the other way. In a flash, the mysterious woman disappeared, swallowed whole by the darkness outside.

Aaron placed one hand on the knob and looked back at Mama Gene.

"Her room's coming out of *your* paycheck," Mama Gene said, baring her yellowed teeth as she spoke.

Stella edged her way toward the kitchen. She had already told Carmen that Roger was dead and their scheme was working. In reality, that was far from the truth. There had to be a way to fix things and get back on track. But before she could think about it, Aaron was already on the move.

He hastened to Mama Gene and touched her elbow. "Listen," he said between panting breaths, panic rising in his voice. "You've got to call the police."

"That's a fine idea. I'm sure they'd love a word with you."

"Please, listen. We have to—"

"You harassed a customer then left my office door unlocked, you idiot." Mama Gene brushed past Aaron and Stella into the kitchen. "Now I have a squatter problem. Where's Will?"

Aaron attempted to follow.

Stella jumped in his way. "Get a hold of yourself."

"When the police come, we'll have nothing."

"They won't come." Stella braced him. "We can handle this on our own."

"But Mama Gene. When she finds—"

"She'll go home soon, back to bed."

Aaron looked at the door and then to Stella. "You know, you're right."

Stella smiled and patted his arm. "Maybe the woman in black did it. Maybe she didn't. Doesn't matter. We'll clean this up and move on."

Theresa quietly came down a few steps with one finger pressed to her lips. Stella waved her over, but Theresa refused to enter the lobby. She crept back upstairs and into the shadows.

Mama Gene and Will returned a moment later. Will winked in Stella's direction. He was still wearing Aaron's blue coat. They joined the others and formed a semicircle around the desk.

In a huff, Mama Gene placed both hands on her wide hips. Before she could speak, the phone in Will's pocket began to ring and vibrate. Despite his supervisor's protestations, he grabbed it.

"Hello?" Will excused himself and headed back to the kitchen. "Now's not a good time. Please stop calling me. Yes. He's gone. I'll explain later. Bye."

When he hung up and turned around, his jaw dropped. Not surprisingly, Mama Gene was right on his heels, ready to ream him out.

Stella placed one hand on the counter and leaned in. *Will's bound to let something else slip about his whereabouts.*

Aaron was behind Stella's shoulder. The gentle hum of the fridge was no match for his deep breathing.

Mama Gene hollered, "This ain't a shelter!"

Will shrugged. "I've got nowhere else to go. If I can't sleep, I can't work."

"I've had just about enough of you."

"Let me work it off. You'll get every penny from me. I swear."

She sized up his T-shirt and sweatpants. "You'll need to change."

Will sprinted back toward the lobby, his swift footsteps echoing up the stairs.

"Can I get some help, please?" an unfamiliar voice called out from the lobby.

"Yes, ma'am!" Aaron called out as he tried to brush past Mama Gene.

"Stop." She put a hand to his chest. "You stay here." She glanced over to Stella. "You go."

As Stella proceeded to the lobby, the light above Aaron's head illuminated the concealer around his left eye.

Mama Gene pointed to his brow. "I told you I didn't want any trouble here."

"This is nothing." Aaron gently touched his cheek. "A box in my closet came down when I—"

Mama Gene flicked her wrist then stormed back into the lobby after Stella. As Stella checked the guest out, Mama Gene wandered around the room, carefully examining the guestbook, the end table, plants, and lamps. She stopped at the breakfast table. "The setup should be almost done by now. What time's the first wake-up call?"

Stella put one finger in the air. "Let me check the book."

Her boss glared at the parlor door. "And why are these doors shut? It makes the room stuffy."

Aaron's head popped out from the kitchen. Theresa and Will tiptoed partway down the stairs. Everyone froze as Mama Gene put her hand on the doorknob.

"Wait!" Stella called.

Mama Gene pivoted while keeping one hand on the door. "What?"

"We haven't, uh, finished..." Stella paused. "We haven't finished killing the spiders."

Mama Gene stifled a sneeze. "Is that why this room is swimming in air freshener?"

"Yes." Stella rushed to Mama Gene's side. "We didn't want it to bother the guests."

"Well, you used too much." Mama Gene thrust open the parlor door. In an instant, she flicked on the lights and moved inside.

Stella glanced behind her, but Aaron, Theresa, and Will were nowhere in sight.

Mama Gene shouted, "What in the world?"

Stella held her breath and rushed inside. Mama Gene stood over the body with a hand to her nose. Stella's stomach sank as she approached her boss. It was all over then.

"What happened here?"

Stella made the sign of the cross. "I've been trying to figure that out."

"Well, I'm here." Mama Gene walked over to the briefcase and opened it. Finding nothing useful, she slammed it shut and kicked it aside. As she moved to exit the parlor, she dragged Stella with her. "And someone's going to pay for clean-up and burial services."

Chapter 7
3 a.m.

Mama Gene returned to the empty lobby. Dark curtains hung limply, and the floor hardly creaked as they walked. The floral scent of the deodorizer breathed life into the otherwise well-lit tomb. Stella carefully closed the parlor doors.

Mama Gene crossed her arms.

"Now you see." Aaron rushed out of the kitchen. "No one can leave. We need to call the police."

Stella moved closer to them and shook her head. "We'll just get rid of him."

Mama Gene smacked her lips. "So, let me get this straight. Theresa's husband"—she pointed to the parlor door with her chin—"was murdered a little while ago. But you don't know who did it."

"How did she figure that out so fast?" Aaron whispered to Stella.

He had no idea that this was Mama Gene's second business. Dead bodies on the property and more questions than anyone would care to answer were her specialties.

"It's late." Mama Gene looked at the staircase. "The guests were probably upstairs. Except suite four."

Stella nodded.

"The only others here were the two of you and Will?"

What if Mama Gene figures the rest out on her own? That was why Stella had had to ask Carmen, the ex-con, to hire some sleazeball out of town for help. Mama Gene knew all the crooks within a fifty-mile radius.

"We were going to call—"

Stella placed one hand on Aaron's elbow and the other on Mama Gene's arm. "We clean it up. Keep this quiet."

"No." Mama Gene removed Stella's hand. "We keep this hotel going."

Stella and Mama Gene locked eyes. She felt stripped and exposed under her boss's unwavering gaze.

"What's happening?' Aaron said.

She turned away from Mama Gene to face Aaron. "Sometimes, Will and I do extra work around here."

"What extra work?" Aaron's head tilted to one side. "Captain?"

"Guests fighting, accidents in the bathroom, car wrecks, 'suicides'—things that are better off buried out back."

"You... you and Will?"

Stella rubbed her forehead. "Remember when I told you about my dead husband's medical bills? The funeral expenses? This is how I've been making up the difference."

"Not anymore." Mama Gene's voice echoed over their shoulders. "I didn't put you up to this mess. I should never have swept Casey's secrets under the rug, and I won't make the same mistake with the rest of you."

When Aaron and Stella turned to face her again, the lobby phone was up to her ear. She told the voice on the other line about the dead man in the parlor and hung up. "Now I should take care of a few things upstairs." Her laser-focused gaze fixed on Aaron and Stella. "Before Hank and the boys get here."

Aaron's eyes flicked back and forth between the two women.

"Come here," Mama Gene gestured for the two of them.

Aaron and Stella edged forward.

Mama Gene pointed a polished fingernail at Stella. "Say a word about my flower bed out back, and your kids will be in foster care tomorrow."

Stella nodded in surrender.

"And you, Aden Camreen," Mama Gene said, pointing toward Aaron. "There won't be another rock left to hide under."

Aaron rubbed his neck. Stella couldn't help but stare at him, a million questions filling her mind.

After grabbing the guest book, Mama Gene hiked up the stairs.

"Hey." Theresa waved from the kitchen for them to join her.

When they entered, Will was inside, leaning against the counter with his head bowed to the floor.

"How?" Aaron's eyebrows raised. "When did you both get down here?"

"We snuck down while Mama Gene was on the phone," Theresa said in a hushed tone.

"What are we going to do?" Aaron asked.

"We lay our cards on the table." Will was still wearing the same T-shirt and sweatpants. "Before Hank and his toy cops arrive."

"What do you mean?" Theresa breathed.

"Which of us found the body, who just attacked a stranger in the lobby, and who wanted us to believe that that Valerie lady did it so we wouldn't see what's been staring us in the face all night." Will pointed at Aaron. "He's a killer."

"Don't be ridiculous." Aaron glared at Will, and his voice deepened. "Which one of us isn't even supposed to be here? You were hiding upstairs, waiting for your moment behind a locked door." Aaron nodded and pointed a finger at him. "I see you. Apparently, you already know about hiding a body around here."

Theresa placed her hand on Aaron's shoulder.

"And you!" Will threw his hands up at Theresa. "I saw you and Roger arguing outside tonight. Looked pretty heated. Someone faxed him a copy of your prenup. Did you ask your boyfriend to kill him for you? Did you promise him cash payment for the job?"

Theresa's jaw dropped.

"We all know." Will picked up Aaron's blue coat from the counter and held it up to Theresa. "This is a nice jacket. Very expensive. How much did it cost you?"

"Mind your own business." She marched over to Will and snatched the coat away. "You think that I don't know about your secret meetings with my husband? Those late-night phone calls. The money you were begging him for."

"You think I'd sleep with your skeezy old—" Will started, but the sounds of sirens in the distance made everyone freeze. Through the kitchen window, Aaron, Will, and Stella could see blue and red lights rushing closer and closer.

Mama Gene's footsteps pounded down the stairs. In an instant, she joined the quartet in the kitchen. She glanced at Theresa and huffed. "Well, look who's here."

Theresa threw on the blue coat. "I came looking for Rog."

Will thumbed around his eyebrow, outlining Aaron's black eye.

Mama Gene snickered. "I'm sure."

The front door flew open. After sizing up Will's attire and growling, Mama Gene bellowed out a cheerful "hello."

Will and Theresa followed Mama Gene back into the lobby. Stella moved to join them, but Aaron gently grasped her wrist.

"Let go." She tugged. Aaron, or whoever he was, had betrayed her. She had no one else to count on to get her out of this situation. *Can tonight get any worse?*

"Let me explain. I haven't been totally honest." Aaron released her. His voice changed to an unfamiliar brogue. "But you haven't either."

"Aden, who are you?"

He cleared his throat, and his usual accent returned. "I let things go too far with Theresa."

Stella tried to pass by him, but Aaron blocked her way.

"A few days ago, I was playing the violin at the bus station for extra cash. Theresa pressed her lips on mine. Then, this random guy punched me for kissing another man's wife."

"I don't care." Stella brushed past him.

"I'm not even mad that you told Will my secret. I understand. We're all scared."

Stella turned around. Aaron's face paled as his shoulders slumped.

Mama Gene called out their names.

"You're my friend," he said without blinking, the lilt in his voice returning. "I'll tell you the truth. I went to Rog while he was waiting in the parlor. I asked him to let Theresa out of the marriage with money to start over. He asked for some water, and I saw him take a check out of his briefcase. I thought that I had gotten through to him. But when I came back, he was dead on the floor."

IN THE LOBBY, FOUR officers and Detective Hank, a large man in a dark-brown coat, were already moving about. A hefty woman with brown hair snapped pictures. An officer with dark skin and sunglasses said the coroner was on his way. As the front door opened again, the chill night air seeped into the room. The once-floral scent had been taken over by chemicals and the whiff of cologne.

Mama Gene gestured for Stella and Aaron to join Will on the wooden bench.

Theresa was behind the desk, watching everything and everyone wide-eyed.

Stella was going to have to make a deal with Mama Gene. There was no other way out of this mess. The problem was, she had nothing left to leverage.

The phone on the lobby desk rang. When Aaron hustled over to answer it, Hank barked, "Stay put!"

Theresa cordially answered the phone instead. She was instructed by the curly-haired officer with a video camera to tell them that there were no vacancies.

While the others were distracted by the call, Will leaned into Stella's shoulder. "Remember. We stick together."

"I didn't promise you anything." Stella scooted away.

Chapter 8
4 a.m.

Stella sat with Aaron and Will on the bench as the four police officers cordoned off the parlor. Plastic wrap on the bottom of their shoes, they brought yellow crime scene tape, rulers, measuring tape, and an enormous white vacuum rolled inside.

Now that she had a moment to think, Stella recognized two of the officers—Nat, with his groomed mustache, and Mario, who refused to remove his sunglasses, even indoors. But the woman was new, and she didn't know the tall officer either. He emerged with Roger's briefcase in his gloved hand then shot to the kitchen, which had become their makeshift base of operations.

With him gone, Theresa glided across the lobby to join them and rested against the wall. Her forehead creased as she gazed at Aaron.

Aaron bowed his head. "Whoever goes first, make sure you tell them about the woman in suite four. Her name was Valerie Marzo. She had reddish hair and was dress—"

Will slapped his knee. "No one is going to help cover for you."

Aaron looked to Stella with earnest, unblinking eyes.

The curvy female officer stopped photographing the doorways to warn each of the staff members against talking, touching, or moving about. They all nodded in submission.

When she had gone, Will spoke softly to the group again. "It's every man for himself now."

Stella rubbed her hands together. *I need to speak to Mama Gene alone and make a deal. She'll want this cleaned up quickly.* At that point, she didn't know which, if any, of her coworkers had killed Turner. Maybe Will had stabbed him in the back and stolen the money. She sucked her teeth. *What happened to it?*

Her mind raced. A while ago, someone had called Will. He'd mentioned over the phone that he'd had "the money" and was ready to go. Besides, Theresa had already accused him of having an affair with her husband, and Will claimed that his boyfriend had left him over it.

Mama Gene walked out of the kitchen with Detective Hank, who was still in his brown coat. Stella said a silent prayer as their boss pointed to each member of the group. Mama Gene was acting as though she didn't already know Hank, Nat, or Mario. As if they hadn't struck secret deals in the dead of night before.

So, who are they putting on this charade for? The other officers? Aaron? Theresa?

Detective Hank asked if he could speak to the wife of the deceased. Theresa straightened, took a deep breath, and followed him back into the kitchen.

The "Jingle Bells" tune sounded from Stella's pocket. Carmen was calling.

Like knives at her throat, all eyes fell upon Stella. She quickly pressed decline and stuffed it into her pants pocket.

The officers returned to dusting and photographing. Mama Gene busied herself organizing paperclips and pens at the front desk. Aaron and Will repositioned themselves to make out what was happening in the kitchen.

Damn! Stella missed her moment. She wished she'd told the police that her kids were on the phone. Then she could have asked to step outside and figured out her next move. But she really did need to call home and check on the kids.

The Christmas melody played again. Carmen. Officer Mario approached, asking her to shut off her phone.

"It's my kids." Stella looked up at him with pleading eyes. "Do you mind?"

He was about to shake his head no.

Her fingertips found his wrist. "Please." Since they'd done jobs together in the past, she hoped he would trust her.

The tune finished. Officer Mario handed her some plastic wrap for her feet. "Make it quick."

"Thank you." Stella slipped the wrap around her boots and hastened to the front door.

After a gloved hand opened it for her, Stella stepped out into the dark. She pressed the contact for Felipe as the door shut behind her.

"Mom," Felipe answered. The grumble of an engine was faint in the background.

Stella glanced behind her shoulder. "Are you all right?"

"We're fine. We left a little while ago."

"The house? Where are you going?"

In the background, she heard Lupe ask for the phone. Felipe said no and returned to the phone. "Tia came and got us. You can catch up in a few days."

"Felipe." All of the muscles in her face tightened. "Put Tia on the phone."

"Mom, just take the bus or something."

"Put Tia on the phone."

After a few muffled sounds through the speaker, Carmen's voice said, "I've been trying to reach you."

"What are you doing?"

"What am I supposed to do? *Your* kids keep calling *me* for help."

"How did you even get here so fast?"

"I came early, just in case you needed backup."

Stella rubbed her temple. "Turn the car around and bring my kids home."

"No. You tipped Marco off and doubled the price."

"What do you mean?"

"Look, Stella. What we planned isn't working out. I'm taking the kids. After you get this all straightened out, join us." The line went dead.

Lights from the lobby illuminated the parking lot and police cars. The curly-haired officer poked her head outside and informed Stella that she had to return. Despite her begging for more time, he threatened to charge her with obstruction of justice if she didn't comply. So she accepted the new plastic booties and went inside.

Her own sister had abandoned her and whisked away her children. Marco could be anywhere, and apparently, the hitman had just doubled his fee. As for the police, they weren't going to turn Stella loose until they got their way. None of them could be trusted. If they found out about her secret meetings with Roger Turner or the Glock in her purse, the situation would spiral even more out of control.

Once inside, Stella ignored the instructions to sit. Instead, she marched straight for Mama Gene. "We need to talk."

She adjusted the collar of her robe. "So talk."

Aaron and Will stared at them with flushed cheeks.

"We need to make some changes to our regular plan."

"Oh, really?"

"Yeah," Stella turned her back and lowered her voice. "You see, there's too many people on shift next week."

Mama Gene huffed. "Well, I still need you. And Theresa, she's in charge of deposits. So either Aaron or Will needs to go."

Stella remained silent. Before tonight, Aaron had always been a good friend. But if Will took the fall, he would take everyone else down with him. She had to do it.

"Aaron," she mumbled as her heart sank. "We'll be fine without him."

"All right," Mama Gene whispered. "He already killed his wife. We can make it work."

His wife? Stella blinked. *But why?*

Theresa and Hank emerged from the kitchen.

"Thank you, Ms. Marzo." The detective's voice sliced through the uncomfortable silence.

Marzo? Stella furrowed her brow. *Is that her maiden name?*

Everyone kept a piercing eye on Theresa as she dodged the cones to find her seat. But when Theresa spotted Mama Gene, her doleful expression shifted. Inches away, she twisted her torso toward the old slave driver. "I quit!" What followed was bellowing, uncontrollable twitching, tears, and laughter.

Chapter 9
4:30 a.m.

Stella had intended to kill one man tonight—one man who could threaten her family. But instead, she'd probably condemned a friend. Yes, Aaron, Aden, or whoever that man was, had lied to her. But everyone had secrets around there. Everyone made mistakes. But if Aaron killed Turner, he would have agreed to bury the body out back the first time she'd made the offer. It couldn't be him. It just didn't make sense.

Yellow tape now blocked the entrance to the parlor and staircase. Stella felt trapped. The officers weren't going to allow her to call home again. Besides, Theresa had already been repeatedly told that she could not leave.

After removing the gold wedding band from her dark fingers, the female officer set herself to a new task, fingerprinting. She laid out the ink and white cards on the front desk and asked Mama Gene and Will to participate.

Detective Hank and Officer Mario were nowhere in sight. Officer Nat was sifting through the closet, getting dangerously close to the concealed Glock.

Theresa slipped into the seat between Stella and Aaron. She could barely make out what Aaron said as he muttered in Theresa's ear. It sounded like "name" and "Marzo" and "paper."

Theresa replied with something about a "cousin named Valerie" and "firm."

Stella braced as the officer in the closet sifted through her coat. She wondered what the penalty was for carrying a weapon without a permit. The Glock would probably make her look guilty. Maybe Mama Gene would turn on her instead of Aaron. Stella knew too much. If that happened, she would end up in the garden with the others. She tried to hold it together as she wondered what would happen to her children without her.

The closet door closed. Her chin quivered, but the curly-haired officer instructed her to move toward the lobby desk. She was next for fingerprinting. That time, she could see the golden badge on his chest—Caleb Lyons.

Mama Gene and Will stood gossiping at the breakfast table as Stella brushed away a tear and stood. But after she followed the cones toward the female officer, she heard her name again.

Detective Hank emerged from the kitchen. He asked Stella to come with him instead. Aaron was called in her place for fingerprinting. Stella followed the detective until she could no longer see Mama Gene and Will whispering to one another.

Hank settled down at the small table beside the window. Officer Mario was already seated. The briefcase, wrapped in plastic with a blue tag, lay on the counter nearby.

Her plastic footing crinkled on the vinyl floor. After filling a glass of water, Stella took a seat on the other side of the men.

"How are you this evening, Estelle?" Hank asked.

The glass tapped the table. "I'm fine, sir."

Mario looked lifeless behind his dark glasses.

Hank placed a small recorder in the center of the table. "Now I've got just a few questions tonight."

The tune, "Jingle Bells," rang out from Stella's pocket. Carmen was calling again. Goosebumps broke out over her arm as she moved to accept it.

"Don't answer that." Hank's eyes scanned the threshold to the lobby then returned. "I've got to be straight with my friend." He leaned across the table and as his voice softened. "Mama Gene wants me to convince everyone that you killed Roger Turner."

"*What?*" Her heart jumped into her throat.

"The alibi you're about to tell us about, working here and not seeing him. Well, Mama Gene told us about your Marco Bolzano problem."

"We already know about the illegal gun in your purse too," Mario said.

The music stopped.

Hank continued, "You asked Roger Turner for his help. And when he turned you down, you decided to kill him."

Stella's body felt weightless. She was either going to sink through the floor or float away through the dusty window.

"Help me help you right now." Hank's voice was eerily upbeat. "Mama Gene likes you. She keeps hold of good workers by blackmailing them. You should know that by now."

She gulped the water dry. "What do you want from me?"

Hank sighed and scanned the threshold again. Next, he got up and knelt beside her. "I need you to point the finger at Mama Gene."

Stella shook her head in disbelief.

"Say that you were forced to stay and help."

"Don't do this," Stella said, her pulse racing. "You know I can't."

"Your fingerprints are all over the place." His voice became more soothing with each syllable. "Heel marks in the parking lot, ashes out back, and the phone log between you and Turner. One of his very last calls came from you."

"Go on."

Hank took a seat back at the table. "When we hit record, say that you found Turner dead in the parlor. You were offered money to help dig a plot out back."

What choice do I have? Stella exhaled. *But this might work.* Aaron would be spared. She could call her sister back and make sure the kids were on their way home.

"Don't look so glum. We all know Mama Gene is a killer, just not tonight." Hank scoffed. "And anyway, no one would ever believe that scum like that was innocent."

Stella's brow tightened. "You know about all that?"

"We're cops," Mario said.

"And what's so different about tonight? Why now?"

Hank threw up his arms. "When the table gets too hot, sometimes it's best to walk."

"Is that why the other two officers are here? Do they also know about the bodies in the garden that you both helped to cover up?"

"Estelle." Hank leaned across the table. "Focus."

Stella nodded in surrender. "I just could never imagine Aaron killing someone, especially his wife. He never told me that she was his wife."

Both men looked at each other and shrugged. She needed to be more careful with her words.

"Aaron?" Hank questioned. "That red-headed pencil out there killed his wife? You sure? How'd you find out?"

Stella felt ready to explode into a million pieces. "Let me get this right. You want me to say that Mama Gene killed Turner?"

"No," Mario replied.

"Stella, pay attention." Hank's voice turned soft and slow. "You're going to say that you were last to see Turner's body. Will and Mama Gene came in before you. Okay?"

"If you try to blame Will," Stella said, her voice growing more frantic, "he'll tell the truth about you and this whole operation to anyone that will listen."

"Don't worry about Will. He's next."

"Are you ready?" Mario put a hand on the recorder.

Mama Gene had turned on her. If Will was blamed, he would too. Things had all gone so completely wrong. She would be blamed for a murder that she did not do. And Carmen would have to keep the kids until she got out of prison. *It could be years.*

Hank took her glass away and set it on the counter. "File for unemployment tomorrow. Maybe we could even talk about Bolzano next week. How about that?"

"We'll start with your Miranda rights after you agree to answer some questions," Mario said. "You know what to do."

"I'm ready." She nodded.

Mario pressed record, and the little gray wheels began to spin.

"Estella Gonzales," Hank stated. "Do you hereby swear that your statements are voluntarily and of your own free will, with no threats, coercion, or promises of—"

The female cop entered the kitchen. "I'm sorry, Detective."

Mario pressed stop.

"What is it, Marie?" Hank asked. "You should know better than to interfere right now."

"I do. But the guests upstairs are getting restless and upset. One of them says that she has to see Stella right now."

Stella pointed to her chest. "Me?"

"Yes. She claims that she found the bag that you've been looking for."

Hank waved an arm. "Take care of it, and don't come in here again."

"I would, sir. But she and some of the others have their lawyers on their phones already."

Hank glanced at Stella. "Come right back."

What now? Stella's wobbly legs managed to rise. She stared at the officer, whose badge read Marie Kovar. The officer smiled and invited her to come with her. The two women walked into the lobby side by side.

Stella was safe for a moment but just that. Her entire world was crumbling.

Chapter 10
5 a.m.

Stella watched a gurney wheel from the parlor to the front door. *Farewell, Roger Turner. Someone must have really hated you.* Or maybe someone like her had been that desperate for the money. The sun was rising when Nat closed the front door behind him, ending Stella's view of the ambulance.

Before Officer Kovar led Stella up the stairs, Mama Gene handed over the key to her office. Meanwhile, Mario called Will into the kitchen. Aaron and Theresa sat on opposite sides of the bench.

"This way, please." Kovar brushed her shoulder and proceeded up the stairs.

Mama Gene's fierce gaze burned into Stella's arm as she grasped the railing. The plastic booties covering her shoes slowed the climb.

If she kept to her agreement with Mama Gene, Aaron would be blamed for the murder. Then she would get in trouble for the Glock in her purse. Plus, Marco Bolzano would still be a threat to her family. No. Stella had to follow Detective Hank's lead now and point the finger at Mama Gene. Then she would be free. Plus, he'd offered to help get rid of Marco. She would have to be crazy to refuse.

Stella reached the last wooden step with a knot in her stomach. Felipe and Lupe were better off in California. She needed to call Carmen and thank her.

Officer Kovar never looked back. Stella stared at her short brown hair as the stairs creaked under them, reassuring the woman that Stella was close behind.

At the top of the stairs, the door to suite six gusted open, and an old man in a green bathrobe stepped into their path.

"May I help you?" Stella asked.

Officer Kovar turned to face them.

"You certainly can." He scowled at Stella. "I have to go to work today. I asked for a wake-up call at five this morning. I should be dressed and having breakfast downstairs by now."

Stella intended to apologize, but Kovar interrupted. "Sir, please go back to your room and wait."

"I need—" His false teeth slipped out, and he shoved them back into place before continuing. "I need to be getting on the road. You can't keep me here."

Kovar jumped in front of Stella. "The roads are all blocked. Wait inside."

"What's going on? Wildfires out back. People screaming at all hours. A knife fight in the yard. I'm being held against my will!"

Kovar grasped one of Stella's shoulders and guided her forward, away from the old man.

The door to suite six slammed with a thud.

When Stella reached the door to Mama Gene's office, it flew open. There in the center of the room was another odd figure. The woman from suite four. She stood with her arms crossed in a dark-blue jacket with unmistakable gold lettering.

FBI?

Kovar gestured for Stella to go ahead. After she stepped inside, the officer left her alone with the agent, shutting the door behind her. The door locked from the outside.

What in fresh hell was happening now?

"Hello again, Stella." The agent spoke with a half smile.

"Your coat... Are you really FBI?" Stella moved to take a seat on the blue-plaid sofa.

"Yes, but don't sit down. Don't touch anything."

"I didn't kill Roger Turner."

"We know." She approached. "I wanted to talk to you about your employer."

"Mama Gene? She didn't kill him. She couldn't have." Stella needed to keep her thoughts in her head. *Mama Gene would have been much more meticulous and methodical.*

"Maybe not tonight. But there have been other incidents. Accidents."

"What are you talking about?"

"Stella, I'm Agent Simone Bridge with the Federal Bureau of Investigation. I'm prepared to offer you full immunity and entrance into the witness protection program if you testify against Eugenie Moore and Detective Hank Ballard."

"What?" Stella's breathing slowed as her jaw dropped. The "Jingle Bells" tune rang from her coat pocket. Felipe was calling, but the agent demanded that she turn it off.

A shadow appeared underneath the doorway. Kovar must have been nearby.

After a long pause, Stella put her phone on vibrate. "Are you serious?"

"Quite."

"I have two children."

"We know."

"And all that I have to do is tell you about this place?" Stella felt a weight lift off her shoulders. *Let the FBI sort this mess out.* She needed to get to California.

The agent handed Stella a gold badge from her pocket. After tucking her phone away, Stella examined the badge. It looked real enough. If not, Stella was either going to jail or into her grave before breakfast.

She handed it back. "How soon? When would me and my kids get to leave?"

"Let's talk first."

"What do you want to know?"

"My colleagues should be here soon." Agent Bridge turned her back to Stella and moved toward Mama Gene's desk. "There's a procedure for this and everything else."

She hoisted the same blue duffel bag from before from under the window. The tight muscles in her arm flexed as she raised it high in the air. "In the meantime, you can tell us about the money I found. There's a check made out to you too."

A knock came, followed by the twist of the door lock. The office door eased open then Kovar stepped inside. Agent Bridge laid the bag on the ground and unzipped the top. Stella peered down and saw that sweet pile of money that Turner had promised her.

Suddenly, it occurred to Stella that if she wanted their help, the first person that she would have to destroy was herself. But she was innocent—mostly. She looked down and noticed that something leather had been stuffed into the duffel bag with the money.

That's Will's coat!

Chapter 11
Sunrise
6 a.m.

Mama Gene's office started to spin. The old wooden floor could collapse any moment, yet Stella was not allowed to sit down. She couldn't leave. The door was locked. She couldn't use her phone to call for help. Her world tilted. She couldn't pretend this was just another day at the hotel. No one downstairs could be trusted. The Glock was in the downstairs closet.

"Stella." Kovar snapped her fingers. "Are you okay?"

Stella clutched her chest. "I need to sit down."

Agent Bridge dragged the desk chair across the room past Will's brown coat and the duffel bag with Roger Turner's money. "Here you go."

Stella sank into the seat and tried to catch her breath.

Bridge hunched beside her. "There's one more thing. If you had something to do with the death of Nicholas Lavelle, we may not be able to work together."

"Nicholas Lavelle? He's dead too?"

"He was strangled at the firm. Someone came from behind with a belt. Cleaning lady found him." Kovar knelt and removed the plastic wrapped around Stella's boots. "We thought that Mama Gene might have been involved. That's why we sent Bridge in advance. The rest of the team's not here yet."

"I never met Nicholas Lavelle."

Bridge frowned. "He was writing you rather large checks."

"Mr. Turner usually paid me with checks from Nicholas Lavelle. He promised me cash after his divorce."

"This new one came directly from his account."

Stella shrugged. *Was Turner going to pay me double tonight? With cash and a check? Not likely.*

Kovar's voice sweetened. "Paid you for what?"

Of all the offers tonight, the agent's was the best one. Stella made up her mind. "Turner wanted information on his wife, Theresa. She was cheating, and they had a prenuptial agreement."

"How do you know that?"

"He told me about the prenup over coffee. Said he needed proof, photos. Theresa would get nothing in the divorce if he had proof, and Roger would give me the other half of the money in cash. But I couldn't. My son was getting suspicious. So I just told Mr. Turner what I saw and when."

"He was paying three thousand dollars for that?"

"Yes."

"Outside in the woods, there were footprints and a fire." Bridge passed her three clear plastic bags, each with strips of paper inside. "Someone didn't have time to finish destroying the evidence."

Stella examined the bags. The first one was half of a charred piece of paper. It looked as though Theresa's name was at the top. Lots of lines and writing. *Could this have been Turner's divorce papers?* The second bag was a photo of Theresa and Aaron, their hands wrapped around each others' waists. Will had probably taken the picture. A cigarette butt sat inside the third bag.

"My money's on the boyfriend." Kovar circled her eye with one finger. "Mr. Turner must have decided to confront him directly."

"No. Aaron's been trying to call the cops all night."

"Could be a guilty conscience?" Bridge said. "Maybe Aden Camreen couldn't stand to do it all again."

"Did Aaron—Aden—really kill his wife?" Stella asked.

"Assisted suicide. She had stage-four cancer," Kovar said. "Aden stole meds from the ER and helped her swallow the contents."

"Oh, that poor man."

"He would have been better off turning himself in," Kovar said.

"But this time," Bridge said, "he takes off with the woman and a whole pile of money. What if they promised Eugenie a big payoff if they could get away?"

"Aaron didn't know that he was being spied on." Stella held up the photo of Theresa and him together. "And Mama Gene would have demanded a much bigger sum if she had any idea what was going on with Theresa's marriage."

"Then who do you think did it?" Bridge asked.

"Let me think." Stella ran her shaky fingers through her hair. In her mind's eyes, she saw her sleeping children riding along the dark highway, and then the image flashed to outside the hotel and the belt near the bushes. "Will. He admitted to the photos. His heels were expensive. He even knew Lavelle's name. But Turner told me that he wouldn't pay for the photos until after the divorce. Maybe he killed him for the money? Planned an escape to Chicago afterward? I know he's got some money troubles."

"Tell me more about Will's problems." Kovar pulled a brass key from her pocket that Stella recognized at once. "I found this key outside, which opened Mama Gene's office door." Kovar nodded to the duffel bag. "Plus, the money was out there behind a tree, wrapped in that leather jacket."

"That's Will's key. Something happened between him and Mama Gene earlier this year. But if he did it, he wouldn't have left his coat lying around. He knows better." But then again, he had been leaving things out in the open lately.

Bridge put a finger to her chin. "What if he, Mama Gene, and Hank were all in on it?"

"It would explain the other two sets of tracks out back," Kovar added. "And why Will would carelessly wrap the money in his coat."

"Doesn't make sense." Stella paused. "Right now, Detective Hank is downstairs offering Will a bribe to arrest Mama Gene for the murder."

"And what about Theresa?" Bridge inquired. "What's she been up to tonight?"

Stella threw her arms up. "Half the time, she's been missing."

"Turner and Lavelle's receptionist, Valerie Marzo, faxed a copy of her cousin Theresa's prenuptial agreement yesterday," Kovar stated. "Turner's very last phone call today was to his wife."

The mystery of Valerie Marzo was solved. Stella exhaled. "Before her shift ended, Theresa mentioned that she and her husband had a date or something planned."

Kovar stated. "So, they met up, and Roger had a copy of the prenup along with pictures of her and Aaron."

"A verbal argument ensued," Bridge continued. "Somehow, Theresa got hold of a knife, and when it was over, she burned everything in the woods."

"The knife. Where did that knife even come from?" Kovar put a hand on her hip.

Stella squeezed her eyelids shut for a moment. These two women didn't have all the pieces together. Stella had some power to play there. "The knife came from a restaurant—Ammaliatore—nearby. I met Roger Turner there for coffee. All their dishes have a silver swan on the brim, and Will works there."

Bridge crossed her arms. "So we're back to Will as the killer."

"Will robbed Mr. Turner, hid the money in the woods, then decided to kill him."

"Another problem." Stella raised her hand. "The prints on the body are going to match Theresa and Aaron."

"And why is that?" Bridge asked in a tense voice.

"They touched the body after we all found Roger Turner, you know, dead."

"Christ!" Bridge exclaimed. The walkie-talkie on her shoulder clamored and rustled. She moved to the window before responding.

"There's only one way to sort out this killer," Kovar said.

Stella shrugged. "How?"

"Put the money back and see who goes for it."

"Then you'll help me and my kids?"

"Not quite." Kovar adopted her friendly tone once more. "You still have to give us something."

"But I told you what I know."

"Sorry, Estelle. It's got to be something that will help our case against Hank and Mama Gene."

"And we already got into the 'broken' elevator and found some interesting stuff, like the hotel's guestbook. So you've got to do better," Bridge added.

Images of Carmen driving away, the Glock, Roger Turner's lifeless body, and Casey's corpse in that shallow grave she and Mama Gene had secretly dug flooded Stella's thoughts. She didn't know how many more lives she would have to destroy to save her own. She'd already lost count of how many times she'd offered to throw her coworkers to the wolves tonight. She was becoming sour and manipulative just like that beast from hell downstairs.

Kovar listened to some chatter from her walkie-talkie. "The team's here. You want to meet us downstairs?"

"Funny." Bridge gently pulled Stella to standing. "Think I'll join you on the stairs instead of my rope ladder this time."

"What's going to happen?" Stella's eyes darted between the women.

"Nothing right away." Bridge released Stella. "Don't say a word. Understand?"

Stella had to make a stand. It was now or never. She made a stern face and used her meanest mama voice. "No."

"Excuse me?"

"I'm not helping you. I'm not telling you anything else until we make a deal."

"We already have a deal." Bridge dropped the bag. "Protection and immunity for your testimony against your employer."

"Aden, Theresa, and Will go free too."

"No." Bridge shook her head. "No way."

"We can keep you safe from Marco Bolzano." Kovar's eyes locked with Stella's.

"Roger Turner was just like Mama Gene and Detective Hank, getting others to do his dirty work and then casting us off when we're no longer needed." Stella breathed. "I'm just as guilty as they are, running and hiding from the truth. We all had a hand in his death tonight."

Kovar placed a gentle hand on her shoulder. "I know that you fe—"

"Don't go there with me." Stella jerked free and positioned herself in front of Bridge. "You want my help? You want to take down Mama Gene and Hank? Then we all get a way out of this sinkhole. Those are my terms."

Chapter 12
That Blinding Light
7 a.m.

The hotel closed around Stella much like her coffin would if the risk didn't pay off. For the kids, Stella had managed to survive at Mama Gene's crooked hotel for nearly ten years because she knew how to keep her mouth shut. She'd looked the other way, followed instructions, and maintained her family day after day. But with Felipe and Lupe out of harm's way, Stella had nothing left to lose. Life, jail, or death. The best of her would go on.

"Okay." Bridge moved around Stella and stopped in the center of the room. "You want to negotiate?"

"I do."

"Final offer," Bridge began. "The others—Aden, Theresa, and Will—get immunity. But witness protection is off the table for you and the kids."

Kovar positioned herself beside her colleague. "Think before you answer. You'll have to publicly testify, and Marco will know where you are."

"He does have a criminal record. But he also has a right to see his child. The court would probably grant him supervised visitation."

Stella leaned her back on the door. Marco could follow her to California. *How am I going to explain this to Lupe?*

Bridge's shadow washed over Stella. "It's better to take our deal and not go to jail. If you do, Marco would have a chance at full custody for young Lupe."

"I changed my mind," Stella snapped. "We need to get into witness protection."

"What about the others downstairs?" Kovar asked Stella. "You don't want to help Will, Aden, and Theresa anymore?"

Bridge shook her head. "Too late. Help us and get immunity, or you and Mama Gene will be cellmates."

Stella got to her feet. "All right." In that moment, a tiny white lie was required. "I'll do what I should have done before Lupe was born. I'll meet with Marco to discuss our daughter. Maybe we can work something out, in daylight, in a public place?"

"After you surrender the illegal firearm in your possession?" Kovar said.

Stella laughed. "Yes. You can have that too."

Bridge opened the office door. "Then let's go."

Kovar picked up the duffel bag and passed through the threshold, and Stella followed. In silence, they walked down the hallway. A few of the guests were at their doors, but two agents in uniform prevented their exit.

Over their grumbling voices, Stella heard Mama Gene's roar from downstairs. "I'll get you!" There was a cacophony of moaning and yelling. "You betrayed me! Stupid kid!"

Bridge waved and instructed Stella to follow her down the stairs. With Kovar at her back, Stella soon found herself at the bottom of the lobby staircase, watching the backs of Hank, Mama Gene, Mario, and Nat being taken out in handcuffs amid a sea of FBI jackets. As the dirty cops and Mama Gene were led outside, Stella could make out the sun's rise above the tree line. An agent closed the front door behind them, silencing their outraged cries and shutting out the light again.

If things had turned out differently, Stella might have been the one carried away in that festive butterfly bathrobe. She was becoming more like them than she cared to admit—their selfishness, their disregard for those around them, and their deception.

Kovar whispered to another agent resting behind the desk.

Bridge joined in their private chatter then put a hand on Stella's shoulder. "Looks like we may not need you after all."

"Why?" She shirked away.

Over her shoulder, she heard Will's voice. "Because I drew them a map of the garden."

Stella turned to see Will, Aaron, and Theresa sitting on the bench, glaring at her. "What have you done?"

"That guy, Officer Lyons. I drew him a map. In red dots, I marked out the spots that Mama Gene liked to use as a graveyard."

Will had saved his own hide and thrown everyone else to the lions. In the end, Stella couldn't blame him. She'd intended to do the same. *But did Will kill Roger Turner?* Maybe he'd cooperated to get a lesser sentence. *Look at him smiling like he just won the lottery or something.* Roger's widow and her lover, on the other hand, looked like turtles retreating into their shells.

Kovar laid the tagged duffel bag on the front desk and asked Aaron to follow her into the kitchen. When he passed by Stella, she reached out and gave his arm a squeeze. "You were my only friend in this place too."

He winked at her and smiled. "See you soon."

Stella's mind flashed to the last image of Casey winking and saying goodbye in the same manner.

Kovar called Aaron inside again, and he disappeared.

Casey had disappeared like that once. One minute, there. The next, gone. Will knew nothing about it. In fact, no one but she and Mama Gene did.

Two hotel guests tiptoed down a few steps. The agent placed Will's coat and Roger Turner's check beside the duffel bag on the desk then directed them to return upstairs. Will's blue-eyed gaze locked on his coat.

Stella kept one eye on Will as she slid into the seat beside Theresa.

"Think we will see him again?" Theresa asked, looking toward the kitchen.

"Don't know," Stella replied. "But what I do know is that Will isn't going to have his coat returned or that pile of money."

Will shrugged. "I can always get another coat. Since Mama Gene will be in jail, she won't be able to collect the debt I owe her. I'm free."

"What debt?" Theresa asked.

"What does it matter?" Will scoffed. "I 'borrowed' some money from her safe earlier this year. She caught me. She wanted every penny back with interest. But not anymore." He chuckled.

Stella glared at him. "Aren't you at least sorry for killing someone tonight?"

"My conscience is clear."

"Come on, Will. You had a key to a locked office for a hiding place. There was blood on your arm. The knife even came from the café where you work."

"How do you think they got hold of one of Rog's checks?" Theresa asked. "Where did that even come from?"

Will chuckled. "Do you want to tell her?"

She turned toward him. "Tell me what?"

Stella exhaled. "That we've been spying on you and Aaron. Your husband was paying Will and me for information and pictures to prove that you'd been unfaithful. You'd get nothing after the divorce." She pointed at the duffel bag. "That money right there was supposed to go to me."

"Funny how you were telling me to mind my own business earlier." Theresa's voice pitched until an agent told her to hush. "You two-faced snake."

Stella bowed her head for a moment. "Your husband came here tonight because I asked him to. But before I could even talk to him, Will stabbed him in the back and robbed him."

"I did not kill him."

"Listen," Stella said. "I made a deal for all of us to have immunity. We're all getting out of here. But you owe each of us an apology, Will. You lied. My sister came and took my children away. And worse than that, you ended a man's life with your own hands."

"Immunity?" Theresa perked up. "I need to tell Aaron. I need to see him." She rose and followed an agent into the kitchen.

Will scooted over to Stella. "I took the same deal. We get immunity for turning on Mama Gene." He leaned over to meet Stella's gaze. "But I did not kill Roger Turner."

"You saw him in the parlor, killed him, took the money, and hid it in the woods. There's your coat with the money, and we both saw the tracks in the woods."

"Hang on. I saw Roger Turner outside arguing with Theresa before he came inside. He threw a copy of their prenuptial agreement at her before she stormed off. So I took my chance. I begged him for some money, and when he wouldn't give it to me, I took it then stashed it in my coat."

"How did your knife end up lodged in his back?"

Will's eyebrows pinched together. "When we were outside, we saw three sets of tracks, remember? But only one could have been mine."

"The second set was probably from the FBI finding the money you stole."

"And the third belonged to the killer—you, Aaron, or Theresa. I left the knife beside the money. One of you came along and found it."

Stella tucked her chin. "You saw my gun. If I was going to kill Roger, I would have shot him."

"Maybe. Or maybe you got so mad that Roger was stiffing you for half the money until after the divorce that you wanted him to suffer."

Stella nodded. Will was making sense. "He must have written me the check after you stole the cash."

"Probably. But if you didn't kill him, that leaves Aaron and Theresa."

"Aaron wanted to call the police as soon as we found Turner's body."

Will smirked. "You know what that means then."

One of the agents appeared and ordered Theresa back to the bench. She sat down on the far side of the bench beside Will and began to cry.

"Did you tell him?" Stella asked.

"No," Theresa mumbled. "They're still talking to him. They wouldn't even give me a minute."

Will tapped her knee. "They're trying to get him to confess to your husband's murder. It's best to let the FBI do their job."

Stella scooted closer, certain Theresa's tears were an act. "Did you start that fire out back?"

She pointed her chin toward Will and snorted. "I'm not talking to you."

"It doesn't matter either way." Will shrugged. "You can tell us. You're getting double immunity."

"Yes. I started the fire." She straightened and dried her eyes.

Will mouthed, "Hers is the third set of tracks."

"Theresa, when you came back, you found Will's coat, the money, and the knife, didn't you?"

"Rog showed me the prenup and some photos of me with Aaron," Theresa said, her face turning fierce, "who's also been trying to break up with me. The divorce papers were sitting in his safe at the firm. I was going to end up with nothing." Tears moistened her cheeks.

"So that's where you went when you left for Roger's law office?'

Will interjected. "What exactly was your plan? Convince Aaron to go on the run with you?"

She sat up. "I did it for the people I love. Like Val, my family. Rog barred her from getting any other job besides being his receptionist. We were all trapped by his money and power."

Theresa had strangled Lavelle with a belt then stabbed her husband. She didn't plan these events very well. But soon enough, she'd be free to go on like the rest of them. Each was desperate, guilty, and had secrets to carry. Each experienced widowhood in some form, including Will, who was grieving the loss of his partner. And each was going to get the second or third chance to start over. Despite Stella's efforts, that was all thanks to Will. *Why did he even do it?*

"What do we do now?" The question bubbled over until Stella couldn't keep it in.

"We sit here until they tell us otherwise." Will stretched on the bench.

"Why did you do it? You got immunity for yourself, me, Theresa, and even Aaron. You tried to make me believe he was guilty the entire night."

He gave Stella a sidelong glance. "Just for the record, Aaron is not your only friend."

A sea of blue uniforms emerged from the kitchen, Aaron in tow. Stella rose to greet him when she observed the silver bracelets around his wrists. He was being escorted to the front door. Before being pushed out the threshold and into the sunlight, he mouthed a "goodbye" and waved with a few fingertips.

Stella had to raise a hand to her eye to block the sun as Aaron was paraded through the parking lot.

"Where are you taking him?" Theresa pushed through the crowd and bellowed.

An officer gently nudged her back toward the bench. The lobby door closed again.

Stella scanned for Kovar or Bridge among a dozen new faces. When she found Bridge coming from the parlor, she called out. "What about our deal?"

Bridge approached. "The deal that we made—"

"The double deal," Will corrected.

Bridge cleared her throat. "Right. That was for what happened on this property. Aden understood that and complied."

"Aden?" Theresa and Will asked together.

"Aaron and Aden—same guy." Stella flicked a hand in the air to get them to stop. "Try and keep up."

"He'll get a fair trial, and justice will be served."

"What exactly was his crime?" Will asked.

"Mind your business." In the corner of her eye, Stella could see Theresa sliding to the other side of the bench, angling herself toward the staircase. In that moment, she also came up with a new idea to leverage Aaron's freedom—tell them where Casey was buried. "I have a proposition. Another deal that will help Aaron—Aden."

Bridge shook her head. "You can't help him anymore."

"There's one body missing on Will's map. Mama Gene dug another grave that only I know about. I'll show you where it is *if* you let Aaron go free."

Will nudged her shoulder. "Who is it?"

Stella ignored the question. "Bring Aaron back, and I'll take you there."

Two other officers approached the bench and asked Theresa to stand. After she did, they wrapped another set of silver handcuffs around her wrists and began reading her Miranda rights.

"What are you doing?" She jerked away.

"Yeah." Will got to his feet. "Leave her alone."

"As I said," Bridge explained. "our deal only covered this location. Theresa is being arrested and charged for the murder of Nicholas Lavelle."

"No. Let me go!" Theresa cried as she was dragged away. "Stella. Stella. Help me!" Her voice carried as she was hauled out the front door into the light. "Please!"

Stella could have helped her with the knowledge of Casey's gravesite, but then another criminal would have gone free. Granted, Theresa wasn't a bad person. Circumstances and desperation had forced her hand.

The lobby door closed for the third time this morning. Theresa, like Mama Gene and Hank, needed to face justice. But Aaron was different.

"Tell you what," Bridge said, toe to toe with Stella, "if you tell me where the last body is buried, the two of us will pay a visit to Marco Bolzano together."

"Who's Marco?" Will inquired.

Stella whipped her head toward Will. "Will you be quiet!" She took a breath and turned back to Bridge. "Bring Aaron back."

"Give up the body, and I'll go with you when you talk to Marco about sharing your daughter."

It didn't take long for Stella's lie to come back and bite her. She remembered their previous deal—immunity or sharing a cell with Mama Gene. If Stella didn't help, if she didn't agree to meet with Marco, it would be a very long time before she saw her children again. Her jaw must have hit the floor.

"People behind bars still get phone calls, letters, and visitation." Bridge waved for Will to stand. "You're not betraying anyone. You're making sure that everyone here finds some peace."

Kovar came from behind and touched Will's shoulder. "Ready?"

"Ready for what?" Stella gasped.

"Yeah." Will nodded.

"Where are you taking him?"

Will faced Stella. "Witness protection. If Mama Gene or any of her goons ever find me, well, you must have heard her." He wrapped Stella in a hug. "Can I have your gun?"

"No." She laughed. "I have to turn it over."

He released her.

Kovar tapped Stella's shoulder. "You should get ready to go too. It'll be better if the guests didn't see you." Uniforms were already laying down a lane of orange cones from the staircase to the front door. They were preparing a checkout process for the guests.

Stella nodded, but she wasn't ready for Will to go yet. "What about Tyson, acting school, your play?"

Will shrugged. "I'll figure something out. I hope."

Without another word, Kovar led Will into the sunlight.

Stella was the last one standing in the lobby. Voices behind her were getting ready to allow the guests to file downstairs.

"So, what it'll be, Estelle?" Bridge asked. "If I find another body around here on my own, it won't be a good thing for you."

Stella nodded. "Below the front step, around where the broken gravel is spread. Look down there."

"Who is it?"

"Casey. She was here when I started. Cute kid. But she figured out what Mama Gene was up to. When she tried to go to the police, Mama Gene poisoned her. She forced me to help bury Casey, said that me and my kids would be next if I didn't. The very next day, Will started working here."

"So why isn't Casey buried with the others out back?"

"Mama Gene thought I needed the reminder every day." Stella found her purse in the closet and handed it to Bridge. "In case you haven't noticed, she enjoys walking all over her employees."

Bridge told another agent to start digging up the gravel while Stella put on her coat.

When she returned, Stella continued, "About Marco—when I found out I was pregnant with Lupe, I tried to find him and tell him. Instead, I met his wife, found out about his past, and ran."

The hotel guests were descending the stairs one by one between the marked cones. Stella turned and buttoned her coat.

"We know." Bridge handed Stella's Glock to another uniform. "But you're not alone this time." She zipped up her coat. "Let's stop by your place and check on the kids."

Stella cleared her throat. Bridge and the rest of them didn't know everything. They didn't know about her adopted sister, Carmen. She also didn't hear Stella blurt to Will the fact her children were gone. Stella could say no thank you to Bridge and walk away. Then she and the kids could take their chances and start a new life in California as planned. Marco might never find them.

Stella shook her head. Like Aaron, Theresa, and Will, she was done with secrets and hiding. "Let's just get this over with. I'm sure that you have other things to do."

Felipe and Lupe were safe, and the sooner she found Marco, the sooner she could catch up to her family in California. To start over with some possible supervised visitation for Lupe's father would be better than living on in fear and shame. Better than becoming another Mama Gene.

Stella straightened her collar and tucked the clutch of her purse into her elbow. With Bridge in her shadow, she proceeded out the front door to willingly greet the new morning light.

Don't miss out!

Visit the website below and you can sign up to receive emails whenever Rachel Pinder publishes a new book. There's no charge and no obligation.

https://books2read.com/r/B-A-EHER-NIFUB

BOOKS2READ

Connecting independent readers to independent writers.